MW00513605

HAUNTED TOWN

Tim Nook

Copyright © 2022 by Tim Nook

All rights reserved.

No portion of this book may be reproduced in any form without written permission from the publisher or author, except as permitted by U.S. copyright law.

Contents

Prologue

S he woke up with a jolt, a shriek escaping from her lips. Beside her, the book fell from her husband's hand and landed with a soft thud on the carpeted floor. "What happened? You ok?" He asked, touching her shoulder. At the contact, she jumped up, startled. "Did..did you feel it, Tom?" She asked him in a hoarse voice, looking around the room. "Feel what?" "Something slithering...over ....our bodies." She asked hysterically, throwing the blanket off them as fast as if it was on fire. "Martha, you ok?" Her husband asked, picking up the book and placing it on the bedside table. He turned his focus on his wife who was shaking and had her arms around herself. She turned towards her closet when she heard someone giggling. Of someone young. Like... "MATTHEW!!! OUT OF THE CLOSET NOW!" She shouted, walking towards her closet and filled with rage now. Matt's pranks were starting to get on her nerves now. He had been playing pranks on them for a couple of months now because he wanted to go back to the house they had left three months ago. From Chester to Elmdale, Matthew still hadn't gotten used to it. "Oh

Matt..." She ignored her husband's mumble behind her. He made no move to get off the bed and question their son's unrefined behavior.

Furious, Martha threw open the closet doors. "What is it?" Her husband asked her in 'what-now' voice when she gasped loudly. Matthew wasn't in there. No one was. She swore that she had heard someone giggling but there was no one in the closet.

"That's...." She whispered but stopped when she felt something in the closet or someone who wasn't Matthew just up the top shelves. With her heart beating furiously in her chest, she let her eyes travel upwards. "Wh....." She gasped but the words die down on her lips. As she stared into the dark closet, something jumped down from the top shelf. Beyond terrified, Martha took a few staggering steps back. It was a woman. Kind of. She had pale white skin and jet-black hair with ember eyes which glowed in the darkness of the closet. She had blood red lipstick on, making her lips sparkle in the lamp light from the bedside table. She was eerily beautiful. She looked at Martha just as a wild animal looks at its prey. When she licked her lips, Martha's stomach dropped in horror and she tried to scream. "Mar-" Her husband called her name but stopped when their bedroom door kicked open with enough force. With shivers running down her spine, she turned to look at the person standing in the doorway. He wasn't someone who was there to help them but someone who looked exactly like the woman in her closet. Shaking, Martha took staggering steps back towards her husband who was still on the bed, stupefied. His eyes traveled back and forth between the intruders.

When the guy in the doorway smiled at Martha, she shuddered. "Already hungry, Quinlynn?" The guy intoned mutinously towards the woman from the closet. As if suddenly coming back into his senses, Martha's husband got off the bed and pushed her beside him. "Who are you and what are you doing here?" He asked firmly but Martha could hear his voice quiver. "Its 2am in the night, are you here to rob us?" The guy in the door way chortled. The sound of his laughter made Martha uncomfortable and scared. His laughter was inhumane and there was something in it that she could not point out. "We are here to rob...." The woman, Quinlynn drooled out the words as she stepped out of the closet and into the bedroom. "But we don't need your things. We need something else from you." "Quinlynn, it is my turn. Why are you here?" The guy in the door huffed and folded his arms over his chest. When the woman turned her attention towards him, Martha's husband dived for his phone. He had barely picked it up when the woman moved. Within a blink of an eye, she had him pinned against the wall on Martha's left. Terrified, Martha closed her eyes. "You think you can call for help without us knowing?" Quinlynn snickered at Tom. Martha heard her husband struggle but she could not lift up her eyes to see what Quinlynn was going to do to him. She wanted to scream for help but her voice betrayed her. "Please, take whatever you want but leave us alone." Tom begged the woman. The guy in the door chuckled loudly. "I'm afraid Mr. Reid, we are starving and we need to eat something." "I'll take you to the fridge," Martha blurted out. Tom's face was bulging and swollen as Quinlynn put more pressure around his neck. "Please. I will give you anything you want." Quinlynn laughed mirthlessly at Martha's words. "It is not the food in your refrigerator that we need. Its youu.. ..." She drooled out the word, pointing her forefinger at Tom. Martha ran to pull her away from Tom. Taking a fist-full of Quinlynn's jet black hair, she pulled, causing her to let out a scream which made Martha's blood run cold. Tom coughed and sagged against the wall as he struggled to breathe. The guy kept standing in the doorway as if amused at the scene unfolding in front of his very eyes. Taking the hold of Martha's hands in her hair, Quinlynn turned around. Martha screamed when her hands twisted and she let go. "No one can harm me and certainly not some lowly human being like you." Quinlynn snarled, her pointed teeth visible in the dim lights of the bedroom. Vampire? It was all Martha could think. Letting out a soft whimper, Martha closed her eyes as she sagged onto the floor. "Matt?" She asked Quinlynn hoarsely, thinking about nothing but her son. "Who is that?" Quinlynn replied, narrowing her eyes down at Martha. So they don't know about Matt. He ought to be safe. She thought and took in a deep shuddering breath.

"Open your eyes, Mrs. Reid, you need to see this." The guy whispered just in her ear, his cold breath sending shivers down her spine. She just shook her head vigorously. She kept her eyes closed tight when she heard Tom scream. It was a blood curling scream which made Martha shudder on the floor. "Just like I thought. People from bigger cities taste much better." Quinlynn said cheerfully as Martha heard the sound of her licking her fingers. "Now we have to keep this woman in storage with the others. We are running out of place Quinlynn, stop going for the fresh hunt." The guy was saying, his words sliding out lazily. Swallowing, Martha opened her eyes. Quinlynn and the guy were standing beside Tom who was unconscious on the floor. "Tom??" Martha crawled towards him, tears pooling in her eyes. Just what did the woman do to him? "Tom? Honey?" She patted Tom's cheeks but he made no movement. She gasped when she noticed small holes around his temples. Crying, she tried to shaking him awake. With her hands shaking, she touched his pulse. When she couldn't feel it, she put her ear against his nose. He wasn't breathing either. He was gone. Martha screamed, pressing the heels of her hands against her temple. She screamed for help but no one came. Quinlynn and her partner laughed at her.

"WHO ARE YOU? WHAT HAVE YOU DONE TO MY HUS-BAND?" She screamed at them. They regarded her, amused before the guy stepped towards her. "I will show you." He said, offering her his hand to take. With her tears streaming down her cheeks and anger and fear flaring through her, she spat on it instead. The guy's playful smile vanished in an instant and before she could even blink, he had her pinned against the wall. Martha could see that he was furious now and for some reason, he looked even dangerous than Quinlynn. "Instead of showing you what we do, you should see it instead." He hissed, causing Martha to shiver because of fear. His eyes on her, he pressed his palms against her head. She wanted to kick the guy or try to run but she realized that she was glued to the spot. She could not even try and speak. With a sick smile, the guy closed his eyes. She felt dozens of needles inject into her temples. She screamed but no sound came out of her mouth. That is when Martha felt, all the blood rushing up from all over her body. First her legs gave out but she didn't fall. Then she lost the sensation in her arms. Her head throbbed as if it'd burst open. The last thing she saw was the face of the guy. Net of black veins on his pale skin.

Chapter 1

#1 - Elmdale

"Then I shall have my own room!!!" Simone snorted at her brother's excited voice from the next room. "Yep sweetheart. And you can decorate it however you want." Her mother was saying. Sighing, Simone looked at the bare room she was standing in. With furniture gone, it looked spacious than it had been. Dark purple paint was peeling off here and there. She clenched her jaw to keep herself from crying. She was going to miss this room.

"Honey, are you done packing?" Her mother peeked inside the room ."Yes, I'm done." She replied, her words sliding out lazily. Shouldering past her mother, Simone headed downstairs.

Everything had already been loaded into the truck. Simone hugged herself against the early November chill as she stepped out. "I heard that it snows heavily in Elmdale." Her brother was saying to her parents behind her. They nodded and ruffled his hair before heading towards the car. Reaching the car, Simone turned around to look at the house she had grown up in. It was the home she remembered and cherished for as long as she had lived. Now she was leaving it. Forever.

She felt her eyes burn with unshed tears as she looked over the patio. She remembered sitting there for hours in spring and drawing. Then she looked at the flowers and vegetables in the small garden on the left of the driveway. She remembered her grandmother humming as she had dug and planted the seeds. Simone was leaving it all behind.

"Come on, let's go Simone." Her mother called as she sat down in the passenger seat. "Yeah. Whatever." She mumbled and got into the car. "Jayden, sit back in your seat." Her father said, bonking her brother's head poking between the front two seats. As he yelped and grinned, Simone rolled her eyes and sat back. She took out her ipod and put on the headphones. She closed her eyes to music blaring in her ears. Then they were on their way.

Simone must've had dozed off because when she felt someone shaking her arm, she jerked awake. Her head hurt and she groaned out loud."What?!" She snapped at her eleven year old brother. Instead of saying anything, he rolled his eyes before pointing outside. It was dark, the sky beautiful shades of violet and orange. There were thick trees on the either sides of the road and not a soul to be seen. Or...."That old man tried to stop the truck and now dad wants to know why." Jayden said, curiously looking out at his father making way towards the old man. The truck was nowhere in sight, it must've kept going. Simone stepped out of the car too. At the sound of the door closing, her father looked over his shoulder at her."Simone, stay in the car.""I....I'm fine." "Simone, you should listen to your father." Her mother told her crisply but she ignored her.

"I have tried to stop everyone from moving here." The old man said, pointing his forefinger at the board behind him. It was rusted and bent over. It read 'Welcome to Elmdale' Swallowing, Simone looked at the old man whose form was lighted by the car's headlights. He had a hunch back and wore old worn out clothes. He was shivering a little, she noticed. His gray-white hair were unkempt and long just as his beard. Simone had a feeling that this guy might have been living in the thick trees around them."Why?" She heard her father ask him dubiously. He had stopped some five feet away from the old man."Those who live in Elmdale never see rest of the world again. They are Elmdale's forever." The old man replied, his tone soft and sad. Unconsciously Simone bit her cheek. "Oh. I guess its perfect for us then." Her father said with a smile and turned around.

"The shadows rule Elmdale, sir." The old man called out behind him but Simone's father just waved his hand without turning around. Simone felt hair on her arm rise and her heart stammered. This was surely not a promising start. She wanted to shout to her parents to turn around but when her mother shot her a disapproving look, she swallowed and got back inside the car. The old man kept standing where he was. As the car passed from in front of him, Simone saw him make a cross with his eyes closed. She kept looking at him but the darkness of the looming night swallowed him.

She kept replaying the words of that old man over and over again as they entered Elmdale. It was a small town and rumored to have only three thousand population. It had thick trees around it and hills beyond them. The house they had bought was at the end of street three. Simone noticed that all the houses were dark. There was no light to be seen anywhere. It was just eight pm in the evening. The road and the houses were illuminated by the street lamps alone. Simone did not like it. Beside her, Jayden was quiet too. He was looking around with his eyes wide open here and squinting there. "Ok. I take back what I said. I don't like this place." He announced, causing their father to slam his hand on the steering wheel. "Listen to me carefully both of you." He began, slowing the car where the truck was parked in front of a house. "This is the only place we can live in peace. You will have to cooperate because I don't care if you love this town or hate it. It'll be our world now." With these words, he was out of the car. Simone let out a breath audibly as Jayden sunk back into his seat mumbling God knows what. "Stay in the car. I'll help your dad." Their mother said and got out of the car, leaving Simone and Jayden alone.

Quietly, Simone let herself study her surroundings. All the houses in the street looked the same. A small driveway and a small garden. Two steps towards the main door. A large window to the right of the door and garage to the left. Their house back in the city had been smaller. Her parents had got this one cheap, Simone wanted to know why. There was a road where the houses ended and then thick trees. As she looked at them, her heart jumped in her throat. Someone was peeking at them from behind a tree trunk. She could see a pale face amidst the dark surroundings. Simone squinted and leaned forward in her seat. Yes, it was a face. Taking a deep breath, she got out of the car while she kept her eyes on the peering face. As if noticing her gaze, it disappeared. Against her better judgement, she ran to follow. "HEY SIM!!!" Jayden called out to her but she ignored him. Her brain told her to stop and turn around but she kept going. She climbed up the higher ground swiftly and halted when she reached the first row of the trees. It was dark. She could not keep going. Breathing heavily, she turned back. It had been a stupid idea anyways, she thought. Whoever it was would've disappeared deep in the trees. The sounds of twigs snapping and dry leaves crunching under the footsteps made her stop. "Who's.....there?" She called meekly but was met with silence. Trying to calm her thundering heart, she took one more step back. More sounds followed. "Show yourself." Simone whirled around and squinted her eyes to see in the dark.

"I'm not here to hurt you." Said a weak voice plaintively. It sounded like a guy. Simone took a couple of more steps back. "Who are you?" "It doesn't matter. You shouldn't have moved in that house or in this town." "What....what do you mean?" Simone hugged herself and rubbed her arms. She could her own heart pounding in her ears but she could not run. "Shadows rule this town. No one is safe." She tried to see him but could not. He had hidden himself in the shadows perfectly. "That house you moved into? It's not safe either."

With her mouth dry and legs shaking, Simone supported herself by placing her hand against the thick tree trunk in front of her. "Why is it not – " "Simone!! What the hell are you doing there?" Her mother called her, startling her. She had walked up to the center of the road and was looking at Simone few feet away. She could not see her mother's face. "I'm......" She began. "Go." The guy said and she heard him move away deeper into the forest this time. "Get back here!!!" Her mother said angrily, barely keeping her voice down and turning back towards the house. Simone descended towards the road and stopped a few feet away from her mother who She had her hands on her waist and was instructing the workers to move faster. Slowly, Simone turned to look back her eyes automatically landed onto the road. At the shadow of her mother's.

Suddenly, Simone's throat was dry and a scream was stuck in her throat. It wasn't her mother's shadow. It couldn't be. Desperately, she looked at her mother who was clad in loose white button-down shirt and jeans with sneakers but the shadow......it was wearing high heels with a hat. It was longer too and more solid. And it turned to face her. Simone staggered back and fell on the road, gasping for breath.

Chapter 2

#2 - Spooked

Simone tossed and turned all night in her bed. The image of the shadow was stuck in her mind. Every time she closed her eyes, it was there. Earlier, her mother had looked at her with a sigh and had helped her up. Simone had tried to look at her shadow once more but it was normal then. Maybe I had hallucinated? She thought for the nth time. After that, she had looked at everyone's shadows all through the dinner. Jayden had laughed at her for being spooky for no reason but she was too exhausted and scared to respond. Her parents had promised them a good start and many other things but she had hardly listened. Warnings of the old man and the guy in the forest remained with her.

Simone woke up at her alarm. Rubbing her eyes, she groaned. Her head felt heavy. She had no idea when she had dozed off last night. She parted the curtains from her bedroom window and looked outside onto the quiet street. Curtains were being parted in the house in front of hers and an old man was getting into his car on the house on her left. She smiled. So people really do live here. She thought.

As the sun rose in the sky, everything looked normal but it wasn't. Simone could tell that something was off. She was missing something but what? She had no idea.

After breakfast, her mother dragged her and Jayden into the living room downstairs to help her unpack. Her father had gone to the mayor's office where he had got the new job which paid a little less than his previous. "This place is dead." Jayden mumbled at his mother as Simone was setting up the bowls in the kitchen cabinet. "Jay hon, not you too. It's a good place and we're going to be happy here." She heard her mother sigh. "No, I meant just look outside. There are no birds. No animals like cats or dogs when we're just near the forest." Simone stilled. That was what was missing. The chirping of the birds. There had been no birds at all. "Why would they be in town when the natural habitat is right there?" Her mother smiled and jerked her head towards the thick trees near their house. Simone didn't say anything but kept looking around for shadows. Twice, she felt like she'd seen something from the corner of her eyes but when she turned to look, there was nothing. At about seven in the evening, her father returned.

"How was your day, dear?" Her mother asked him, taking his bag and coat. "Tiring. Too much work at the office but this town is peaceful. I'm sure we're going to be happy here." Simone resisted the urge to roll her eyes at the table. She was watching television with her brother but her ears were focused on her parents' conversation. "I'm glad." Her mother replied. As they made their way up the stairs towards their bedroom, Simone turned her head to look. Popcorn fell from her fingers as her eyes widen. Shadows. Two of them were following her parents along with their own shadows. "Jayden." She whispered, nudging him with her elbow. "Look at mom and dad."Her brother scrunched his face at her and then turned his head to look. "I've seen them all my life. What's different?" He asked loudly. Clenching her jaw, she turned to look again. Her parents were laughing at something on top of the stairs but the shadows were gone. Had she hallucinated again? She wondered.

That night, Simone took out her camera and sat down on the window seat. She focused on the street outside. People were disappearing into their houses, curtains were being pulled and the lights were being turned off. Soon enough, everything was shrouded in the darkness. The only light came from the dull orange bulbs of the street lamps. "I've no idea what the heck am I doing?" She grumbled, turning her cell phone to silent. She waited for about an hour but saw nothing and heard nothing. She dozed off. When her head hit the window sill, she groaned and forced her eyes to open and look outside one last time.

What she saw was going to haunt her forever. The street, it was covered with shadows. Simone gasped and her skin prickled with fear. What the hell was she seeing? She squeezed her eyes close, hoping that they'd be gone and it would be just another hallucination. She opened them up slowly, her heart thudding in her chest. It wasn't a hallucination. The street was covered with shadows. They were climbing up the street lamps, houses and pulling at one and another on the road. Simone staggered back from the window and landed with a thud on the bedroom floor when her legs gave out beneath her. I made a sound. She realized with horror. Sure enough, she saw hands on her window glass. Before the shadow could see her, she immediately lied down on the floor and pretended to be asleep. She was sure that shadow would be able to hear her heart thudding in her chest. In her heart, she counted to fifty and then opened her eyes. It was dark just like it had been. There wasn't any shadow anywhere. Sighing with relief, she got up as quietly as she could and made her way back towards the window.

The shadows were still on the street but they were not running around wild like they had been. Before Simone could wonder why, she heard the sound.Click, clack, click, clack..... Of the heels. The shadows started disappearing into the darkness and the ones that remained on the road parted like waves for the upcoming figure.Click, clack, click, clack.....It was a woman. Simone swallowed. She was NOT a shadow and shadows were clearly afraid of her. The woman stopped just in front of her house. Her back was to the light and her dark black hair shielded her face. She turned to face the front door. Holding her breath, Simone hid herself behind the curtain but kept looking. The woman wore bright red lipstick and her skin was pale. That was all she had noticed when the woman turned her head to look at the window. Right where Simone was.

Chapter 3

#3 - Elm High

"**H**ey SIMONE!!" Her brother shouted, waking her up. She woke up with a jolt. When Jayden threw open her bedroom door, she shrieked causing Jayden to scream in response."Why the hell are you screaming?" He shouted at her."Why the hell did you?" She retorted. "I screamed because you screamed!" Jayden was saying, his face red. Simone let an audible breath, her hand pressed to her chest. "What is so important early in the morning?""You've got a letter. No name, no address just 'For Simone'." Jayden said, making air quotes in the end. "Your name isn't even spelled right."

Scrunching her face, she reached out for the envelope in Jayden's hand. It was yellow with age and rough to the touch. "So.....who is it from?" Jayden said, jumping up on her bed and leaning against her shoulder. She shrugged him off as she opened the envelope. It just contained a square piece of paper. And only two words:

' Remember '- M

"What the heck is this?" Jayden said, laughing. Simone was confused. Who had sent her this and remember what? "Simone, Jayden. Downstairs now! You have to go to school today." Their mom appeared in the door and looked at them, her hands braced on either side of the door frame. "What is it?" She asked them. Jayden was still laughing as he climbed off the bed. "Simone's got a fan." He giggled as he dived out in the hallway from under his mother's arm. "Sim, hon. You ok? When did you go to sleep last night?" Her mother inquired, making her way inside her daughter's room and threw open her closet. Shaking her head, Simone threw the envelope and the note inside her drawer. "I don't remember." She mumbled. And she truly didn't remember a thing about last night. Had she been so tired that she had gone to bed without even writing in her diary or setting out her clothes for school. Her mind was blank. Now this was a first, Simone thought sulkily.

On the first day of their school, their father had dropped them off but starting the next day they were to go by themselves. A van was supposed to come and pick up Jayden while Simone had to ride her bike to her school which was just two streets over. She hated her bike. It was pink and she had gotten it as a birthday present from her parents on her fourteenth birthday. It was almost two and half years ago.

"Remember, try to be nice and make friends." Her mother began and Simone groaned loud enough to show her how unhappy she was anyway. She missed her old schools and her friends. "Hon, you have to try to fit in otherwise you'll be an outcast forever. First impression lasts forever." Her father instructed as he pulled his car just outside the school gates. Shouldering her almost empty bag, she stepped out. Almost instantly she knew that every eye was on her. From the girls standing beside a brand new red car to the boys gathered by the wall and smoking, everyone was looking at her."Brilliant. Too much for staying low." Simone mumbled and made her way towards the gates. Her face down.

"Hey new girl!" A girl called to her. "Have fun honey." Her mother called unhelpfully from behind her as they drove off. "Hey." Escaping was useless and she didn't want to stand out from doing it. The girl who had called out to her was one of the girls standing by the red car. She had jet black hair and pale skin. Her dark blue top and jeans were perfect on her. She was beautiful. Eerily beautiful. "What's your name?" She asked, raising her hand to greet Simone."Uhh.. Simone." Simone stuttered before meeting the girl's hand."Uhh..Simone, welcome to Elm High. I'm Brianna Hoskin." She said, imitating Simone's introduction. Almost immediately, Simone realized that she did not like this girl. "Thank you. Nice to meet you too." She said, resuming towards the gates. To her dismay, Brianna and her friends followed her.

"Hey Bri! Stop bothering the new girl." A guy hollered from behind them causing the others to laugh."Shut up Nathan!!" Brianna shouted back making her friends giggle. Typical teens...Simone thought. I hate it. I hate it here! Simone thought angrily as she looked over her time table. She shared three of her lectures out of seven with Brianna and her buddies who decided to tag along Simone for the rest of the day including the lunch time in a small cozy cafeteria. "Stay with us, you'd never be an outcast." Brianna was saying, biting into her beef burger. How could she eat that much? "And you'd be popular and in the spotlight." Her friend, Jenna said with a wink. "And you'd get to hang out with boys too." Vanessa said coyly. Simone resisted the urge to hit all three of them with her fork.

Rest of Simone's day passed in a blur as she tried to grasp the concepts that were being delivered. She had transferred in the middle of the semester and it was going to be hellish for her to catch up. At the off time, Simone was glad to find out that Brianna and her friends were nowhere to be seen. They were probably in the cheer leading practice as they had told her they'd be. Glad, she quickly made her way to her locker only to find someone waiting for her. It was one of the guys who had been outside the gates in the morning. "Can I help you?" Simone asked, appearing to be unconcerned and annoyed. "Nah, I don't need your help." The guy laughed. "I just wanted to welcome you to the Elm High." "Thank you?" She said, scrunching her mouth to one side of her face. "So how was your day?" He asked her, flashing his dimples at her as he stepped aside to let her approach her locker. "You care because?" "As a senior in this school and someone who is student body president, it is my job to foresee any difficulties that may befall the new transfers." He explained, causing Simone to snort loudly in response as she tried not to laugh at the use of his words. "I had a fine day, thank you." She flashed a forced smile in his direction before walking away. Thankfully, he did not follow her.

It was evening but her house and the street was dark. Her mother worked in the kitchen as Simone and Jayden laid out the dishes on the table for dinner. Simone watched her mother work. She looked happy and she was humming. Something she hadn't heard in more than two years or so. As she studied her mother, her eyes traveled to her shadow. It was dancing. The shadow of her mother was dancing when her mother wasn't. Simone's eyes widen as she tried not to shout in alarm. It brought back the memories from the night they had shifted. She had thought that it was some kind of hallucination but it wasn't like it wasn't just the night before when her parents were going up the stairs. "You look pale." Jayden remarked unhelpfully, making Simone jump in fright. "What?" She croaked out. "Yeah, definitely spooked since we've moved here." Her brother remarked and went back to playing with his fork and spoon. Simone wanted to point him towards the shadow of their mother's but she knew better. As she watched in horror, two more shadows appeared beside her mother's. They were pulling at each other as if they were fighting. "Simone?" She barely heard her mother. "Simone????" Her mother called out to her again. Then the shadows turned. To look right at her. "Hon, what is it? You're pale." Shadows were moving towards her. Slithering from over the surfaces of the chairs and then the table. When they were just a foot away from her, Simone screamed.

Chapter 4

#4 - Strange Messages

"Simone, honey are you up?" She heard her mother's concerned voice and squeezed her eyes a bit before opening them up. She was in her bed and three faces were bent over hers. "What the hell?" She grumbled as she looked at them."You screamed and then you fainted.""Nathan carried you here upstairs, I had no idea what to do.""Why did you scream anyway?"

Everyone asked the questions one after the other but she was too stunned by the presence of the boy from her locker to acknowledge anything else. What was he doing at her house and in her bedroom? Consciously, she pulled her blanket till her neck. Only her face was visible and she was still looking at Nathan, her eyes narrowed. "She is shy." She heard her brother say mischievously."I'm sorry Simone. I was just passing by your house when I heard the scream. I didn't know it was your house but I rushed in anyway to check if everything was ok." Nathan said sheepishly. "Honey, why did you faint? Did you see something?" Her mother inquired, sitting down beside her. Did I see something? Simone wondered but she could not recall. "I don't know. Where was I? I don't even remembering screaming." She mumbled, trying to recall last few hours of her day but she could not. There was nothing. Her mind was blank.

"You sure?" Her mother asked, her forehead creased in concern." Yeah. I am. Where was I and what was I doing?""Oh my GOD!! She doesn't remember! Are you suffering from amnesia or something?" Jayden asked in a horrified tone with his eyes wide and mouth hanging open. Simone bit her lower lip as she looked at one face to another. "I found you in the kitchen. You were collapsed on the floor and your mother was trying to wake you up." Nathan said, confused as he studied her."Thanks for you help, dear. Jayden will see you to the door." Her mother said to Nathan, forcing a smile in his direction. Thank God, her mother had recalled that there was a boy in her daughter's bedroom. Uninvited one at that. As Nathan followed Jayden out of the room, he stopped at the threshold to give Simone an apologetic smile. She just nodded absently, her mind still trying to grasp what had happened to her.

Later that evening, Simone sat down on at her desk and took out her daily diary. Last entry was three days ago. Never before Simone had missed more than a day or two of entry but this time, she had missed three days in a row. Sighing, she held her head in her hands. She hated this place and everything about it. Nothing made sense and her mind was blank. It was just like it had been the night before. Feeling helpless and annoyed, Simone wrote down about her evening.

A week passed without any incident. After her fainting episode, Nathan had taken it upon himself to walk her to every class. She hated it and had requested him to stop doing it but he had shrugged and had pretended as if it was nothing. It should have been nothing but it was. She could feel everyone's eyes on her. Simone often caught Brianna and her friends watching her. She could not read their expressions but she knew that they did not like Nathan's attention on her. When asked why he was doing it, he had simply stated that because she was a new girl and someone he wanted to know better. Simone had scowled and left him in the hallway as she had ditched into the girls' bathroom.

She still believed that she had hallucinated the shadows of her parents and from the night they had shifted into Elmdale. It was on Wednesday when she got another letter. A note which read:

They're onto you. - M

Simone still didn't know who it was. She had kept the previous one and that is where she saved this as well. Two days later, she found a strange entry in her daily diary. One she couldn't remember writing but it was dated the previous night.

I can't sleep, she'd written. I am sitting down in the window and looking out at the dark trees. Cool wind is blowing. Winter is coming. My neighbors are awfully punctual. At exact 9PM, they are turning off their lights and pulling the curtains. I should turn off my bedroom light too. I turned it off. The only light is coming from the street lamp outside. Its a beautiful night. Now looking at the road, I'm sure that I'd hallucinated the shadow there. I must really hate this town but not at night. Its beautiful. I want to.................... SHADOWS! HUNDREDS OF THEM. ON THE STREET. A WOMAN.....

That is where the entry was ending. She had scribbled the last words hastily. She could tell. Just what had she seen? Why the hell she couldn't remember? She decided to stay up this night as well. This time with a camera.

Come morning, her head felt very heavy and she was sneezing. Her muscles ached as if she had ran miles the night before which she didn't recall. As usual. When her mother came to wake her up, seeing her condition she told her that she'd be calling her school for a sick leave. Simone was grateful to her. When she was gone, she drifted back to sleep.

Hours later, her mother woke her up for breakfast. It was 11AM."I need you to take some medicine, shower and eat. Staying in bed won't help you get better." She endorsed. Simon wanted nothing but to stay in bed for her head felt like a boulder on her shoulders but her mother only left when Simon had started showering.

After brunch, she sat pondering over strange entries in her daily diary. She realized that she had written about the shadows once again and had written that she had recorded last night's events but when she checked her camera, it was empty. Confused, Simone sat down on her bed and re-read the entries. It couldn't have been a prank for she recognized her own handwriting. It was then when her mother peeked inside her room."You have a visitor." She said with a secret smile. Simone frowned."Who is it?""See for yourself." Her mother chuckled, opening the door wide for no one other than Nathan. Simon scowled out loud."Wow. Why do I feel like you didn't want anyone to visit you? Let alone me." He grinned from ear to ear as he made his way towards the chair."Keep the door open kids." Her mother said and left."I'm not suffering from cancer or dying that you had to visit me and ditch your classes in doing so." Simone said in an acerbic tone. When Nathan flinched, she regretted it a bit. He was looking out for her and he had been her only friend in two weeks she had been here.

"I just want to be your friend Simone. To know you better.""Is it because I'm the new girl?" She asked politely this time."Yeah, its part of it." He said, scrunching up his nose. In that moment Simone realized that he was cute. "And the other part?" "Well, you're pretty and not like other girls your age in this town." He said, scratching the back of his head nervously. Simone laughed out loud."Guess not many girls talk to you the way I do." She smirked at him."You've seen them. They pretty much want to worship the ground I walk on. It makes me feel uneasy." He smiled and then pointed towards her diary which she still had in her hand.

"What's that?""My daily diary." "Have you written about me in there?" He asked sheepishly, making Simone roll her eyes. Ok, he was cute but annoying. "As if. I write about the stuff that bothers me. Not the details of every minute of every day." She said, placing it away. Nathan kept looking at the diary, a soft smile on his lips. Simone wanted to ask what was he thinking that was making him smile when Brianna barged into her room followed by Vanessa and Jenna.

Simone's eyes widen in surprise as Nathan's narrowed at Brianna." Hey sweetheart. Learned that you got sick." Brianna said, ignoring Nathan glaring holes into her. "And you are here because....?" "Of course we wanted to check up on you. Here, we brought you something." She clapped excitedly and pulled Vanessa forward. She was a girl with sleek light brown hair and small eyes. Simone wondered if she was Asian. "We didn't know which one was your favorite so we got Brianna's favorite instead. Hope you'd love it." She said with a wink as she passed on a box to Simone. Mumbling a thank you, she opened it up. It was a cake. Plain chocolate cake with 'GWS' written on top of it. Simone hated chocolate so she had to force at smile for Brianna who hugged her."It was so boring without you today." Jenna said as the girls flopped down on her bed around her."I don't remember putting up a comedy show or something in the two weeks I've attended Elm High." Simon said sweetly, making Nathan laugh so hard that Brianna threw him a look. "No, sweetie its not. You are new in town. The last new person moved here three years ago so you are special and having you around is different. Refreshing." She said with a wink. Simone raised her eyebrow heavenward.

"Anyway, let Simone rest today. She needs it." Nathan said, standing up and shouldering his bag pack. Brianne rolled her eyes at him but said nothing. One by one the girls hugged her goodbye and were gone. The room felt warmer all of a sudden. Just then Jayden wandered in, still in his school uniform. He waved another envelope at Simone to jumped off the bed in haste to read it."I think you've got an admirer. I really appreciate the old style of sending the messages." Jayden winked at her coyly. Simone smacked his head and pushed him out of the door.

'Stay away from them'- M

That was all the note read.

Chapter 5

#5 - M

Simone tried to remember something which she had to do last night but could not recall once more. This was driving her crazy. Never once before she had forgotten anything. Was she sick? Or was it something because of this town? She dug out her daily diary from her closet but to her dismay, the pages were missing. They were neatly torn out of the diary. The missing pages lead to a huge fight with Jayden which ended with him crying. He had kept on insisting that he did not know that she had been keeping her diary in the closet. Deep down Simon believed him but if it hadn't been him then who had torn out the pages? This is so great!! She thought, pacing her bedroom. I'm going insane!!

"SIMONE...." Her mother called her down the stairs. Biting her lower lip, she made her way down. It was Saturday and her mother had invited two of theirs neighbors over for the dinner. She was taking out her precious china from the cabinets. One they were not allowed to use at home. "What is it?""I want you to drop by your dad's office and give him this lunch box." She had, jerking her head towards the box on the table. "And after that I want you to buy few things from the store. The list of the items is beside the box." "Anything else?" Simone asked, eying the items on the list. So her mother was planning to throw a feast."No. And be back as soon as you are done. I want you to help me in making dinner.""Whatever." Simone grumbled, her mind still on the missing pages of her diary.

Outside the mayor's office, Simon left her bicycle in the bicycle rack and headed towards the steps towards the building. A woman caught her eye. A woman dressed in red and black. Her back was towards her so she could not see her face. Simone stopped in her tracks and studied her. Something was off about her, something Simone could not point out. She had sleek black hair down to her waist and was dressed in red coat and pencil skirt. Her shirt wasn't visible. An old man dressed in a suit noticed her staring. He nodded towards the woman and turned his attention towards Simone."Can I help you, child?" He asked, clearly unimpressed at her gawking. The woman left then, without turning to look at Simone. Click, clack, click, clack.....The sound of her red heels sent chills down Simone's back but she could not tell why. "Young lady, I asked you what are you doing in front of the Mayor's office?" The old man asked again when she kept on gawking at the woman leaving."I.....I...I'm just here to deliver this lunch box to my father." She said, resisting the urge to look at the woman who was at the building doors by now."And what is the name of your father?""Ian Dawson." Simone said, forcing a smile at the old man who was looking at her with rancid disapproval."Ah, the new guy. Hand the box over to me, I shall deliver it to him." "No, its ok. I'll deliver it myself." Simone said hastily. He raised his eyebrow heavenward at her. Without any other word, he raised his hand for the box. Twisting her mouth and clenching her free hand into a fist, Simone handed over the box and turned towards the bicycle rack without a backward glance. What was wrong with the people here? She wondered as she got on her bike.

Ride to the store took even less time. The town was too damn small. As expected, the store was small and the items were piled in the racks which were almost touching the ceiling. Simone caught herself as she tripped over a box just inside the main door."Welcome." She raised her head to look at the person behind the counter. His voice sounded familiar."Can't say that I feel welcomed. I almost tripped." Simone shot back without thinking. The guy opened his mouth to say something but then closed it. He forced a smile and with a small nod, he went back to his work."Great. These people really need classes on good behavior." She grumbled softly as she took a shopping car. As the shopping cart got stuck here and there while she shopped, she kept thinking about the woman she had seen outside the mayor's office and also about the guy behind the counter. When she reached the counter, she studied his face as he scanned the items in her cart. He looked like someone around her age but was tall about six feet. His curly brown hair were messy underneath his blue cap which had the store's insignia on it. He wore a matching shirt which hung loosely on his thin frame. As if sensing her looking, he looked up at her. "Is there something wrong?" He asked coolly. "We've....we've met before, haven't we?" She asked him, watching his reaction closely. He stilled but made no move to match her gaze. "We've talked before and....." She stopped. He was the boy from the woods. The one who had warned her the night they had moved to Elmdale. "Not here." He whispered as he handed her the receipt. "Meet me where we met at five. Make sure there is no one watching.""But...." "I hope that you enjoyed shopping in Elm Store. Welcome to Elmdale." He said in a professional tone, cutting her words.

Simone wanted to stay and make him talk but one look at his face, she decided that she'd rather meet him in the woods. "Thank you." She smiled at him and left. Just outside the store, she ran into Brianna's co. "Oh my, what are you doing here?" Vanessa asked, dressed in all black. It was strange to see them without Brianna. "Just shoppin'." Simone said, heading towards her bike."Cute bike you've got there." She rolled her eyes at Vanessa without turning back to look at them. When she got onto the bike and looked at the girls, she saw Jenna looking at her strangely. The other one had already disappeared into the store. Simone raised her eyebrow questioningly at her. Jenna just gave her a sick smile. Full of loathing and threat. Unconsciously, Simone gulped and turned away. She could feel Jenna's eyes on her all the way till when she turned the corner. What was wrong with that girl?

She was in a daze as she helped her mother. She kept thinking about the guy at the store. At about 5:15 the guests rolled in. Two of them were women in their fifties while one of them was like Simone's mom. After greeting them, she rushed out of the house. It was quiet. Just like any other evening in Elmdale. Sunlight only illuminated the tips of the trees. After looking down the three roads by her house, she ran towards the forest. She didn't stop. She kept running, feeling out of breath as the ground rose higher and higher as she ran further inside the forest. "I thought you wouldn't come." She came to a stop at the voice. She was breathing heavily and her legs ached. "Guests." She rasped and turned to face the guy from the store. He wore casual brown t-shirt over blue jeans. His curly hair were still messy. He had his arms folded over his chest as he leaned against the tree trunk.

"They didn't notice you leaving, did they?" He asked and she just shook her head."Why did you warn me the day I shifted in this town? The shadows....they're real, aren't they?" "Yes, they are as well as demons who control this town." He replied, looking up at the sky. It was turning darker every minute."De...demons?" Simone stammered. "Yes. They are the ones who control the shadows. And everything else around here.""How do you know this?" She refused to believe whatever he was telling her. Shadows were one thing but demons?"I've been here longer than you have. I notice and I remember." He said, pointing his forefinger at his temple. Simone's eyes widen. "You....You are M. You are the one who has been sending me notes." She said in consternation. The guy just smiled faintly. "You told me to remember but I don't know what I should remember." "Demons, they can wipe away your memories. You must've seen or heard something they didn't want you to know." He replied ruefully. Simone swallowed. The missing pieces of her memories, they had been wiped away just like the torn pages of her diary. As realization dawned on her she stepped back in shock. Her legs felt weak. It made sense. If the shadows were real then this all could be true as well. "The woman......the woman in red." She whispered. The guy's eyes widen as he stared at her."You remember?""No but I can't her out of my head. I saw her. Not her face but her back outside the Mayor's office." Simone said, pressing the heels of her hands against her temples.

"Listen to me." The guy said, suddenly quite near and looking scared. "You have to remember. You have to find a way to keep your memories intact. Don't trust anyone." "Not even you?" "No, not even me." He warned. "Listen, I'm Matthew Brown. I used to live in the house you have moved into. My parents....Tom and Martha Brown." He choked at their names and closed his eyes. Simone could see raw pain on his face. "They were killed by the demons three years ago. I.....I...c ouldn't see their faces but I heard their voices." He said dolorously as his gray eyes searched Simone's. "Oh my God." She whispered."You have to figure out something." He said with urgency this time. " All this has been going on for years and will keep happening if we won't stop them.""But how will I figure out who they are?" "Start with the woman in red. And trust no one. No one." He said, placing his hands on her shoulders and squeezing them."You are scaring me." It was all Simone could say before Matt took a couple of steps back and looked behind them. His eyes were wild and his face pale."Shadows. They are here. It can't be." He gasped as they both looked at the shadows storming into the forest. "They must've been keeping an eye out for you. Run. I don't know if I'd be able to help you any more." With these words, he pushed Simone back and ran. He was heading deeper in the woods. Simone watched him go, her heart thundering in her chest as the sky turned darker overhead and the shadows closed in behind her. Simone let out a scream. She was scared, tired and feeling hopeless.

Chapter 6

#6 - Recovered Files

B reathing raggedly, Simone turned to look at the shadows. They weren't there. There was nothing around her but dark trees. The sun had set and there was no light to make shadows. Taking a deep breath, she made her way back towards her house. She stopped dead in her tracks when she spotted Jenna there, waiting for her. She was leaning against her car parked in front of her house. She was dressed in white button down shirt over black jeans. She was looking the other way as she twirled her car keys around her finger. As if sensing her there, she turned to look at Simone. "Where were you?" She asked, eyes narrowed. Simone shrugged and headed for her house. "Hey, I asked you something." "I was just around. Why are you here?" "I wanted to talk to you, mind if I come inside?" She asked, her face giving no clue as to what she wanted from Simone. Sighing loudly and facing her, Simone shook her head. "Sorry, mom has guests over and whatever you need to say can be said here." Jenna scoffed, "I don't know what's so great about you that both Brianna and Nathan can't shut up about you." "Jenna, why are you here?"

Simone bit out the words, impatient to get inside. In the safety of her bedroom. Or maybe she wasn't safe even there.

"Is this page yours?" She said, revealing a folded piece of paper she had in her hand. It was light blue in color. The same color her diary was. Color drained from Simone's face as she reached for it. "Where did you get this?" She whispered. "It was in my locker. I know your handwriting so I knew that it was yours right away." Jenna shrugged. Carefully, Simone opened the page and head for the street lamp to read. She couldn't walk more than three steps. There were shadows. A couple of them underneath the lamp. "You know, thank you." She told Jenna awkwardly as she rushed towards the main door. Inside, she could her the ladies chatting and laughing. As she rushed up the stairs, she could hear the clinking of glasses. It was going to be a long night, she thought. On top of the stairs, she felt something cold around her ankles. When she looked down, she gasped. A shadow. Or a hand of a shadow. Wrapped around her ankle. Stifling a scream, she jerked her ankle and rushed towards the dark hallway as soon as she felt it let go. She dodged into Jayden's room which was dark for he was down with her mother. Catching her breath, she peeked out in the hallway to look for the shadow. Sure enough, it was still there on top of the stairs. Waiting. Despite being scared, Simone realized something. Of course, the shadows could not form where there was no light. They could never follow her into the places with no lights. She laughed skittishly. Why couldn't she think of it sooner? Straightening her shoulders, she threw open her bedroom door and stepped inside.

Her confidence evaporated as soon as she looked at the state of her room. The light from the street lamps illuminated her room but that was not what took her breath away. Shadows were crawling all over the room. They scattered like ants when she came in. Within a blink of an eye, they were gone. Simone knew, she knew that if Matthew had been honest then she would lose this memory. Memory of meeting Matthew and shadows on the stairs as well as her room. She looked down at the paper in her hand. It was just like any other page from her diary with nothing significant about it. At least not what Simone wanted.

Throwing the paper away, she took out her phone and threw open her closet. She knew that she could fit inside just fine. With one look at her room from over her shoulder, Simone got into the closet and closed its doors behind her. It was difficult to sit in there. With so many clothes hanging, it was hard to breathe for her. But she needed to do it. She needed to record everything she had seen in her phone. With her phone being on her all the time, no one was going to delete those files. With no shadows in the closet, she was sure that no one would know about her recording everything. For safety measures, she wrote about her day in her daily diary and neatly placed it on her table. For the demons to find. That night, she placed the camera between her books on the rack. Facing it in a way that it recorded the area around her bed.

Next morning, she woke up with her head feeling like a rock on her shoulders. She could not remember when she had gone to sleep. She couldn't remember anything past making dinner with her mother. Before she could sit up, Jayden barged inside her room. "Please tell me that you have my pictures from the trip this summer." He said, flopping on her bed and practically on her. "Ow! Watch it bozo!" Simone called out. "Please, please tell me that you have those pictures!!" He begged. Rolling her eyes, Simone smacked him on the head. "I transferred those pictures in your tab before deleting them from the camera. What did you do?" She asked him suspiciously. "I accidently factory reset the tab." He said, biting his lower lip. Simone felt as if he was going to cry any second now. "Accidently or purposely?" Simone retorted. "Does it matter?" "Yes, it does. Now I will have restore the files from the camera's memory card. It's a headache and my head is already killing me. I feel like I haven't eaten in days!" She said, glaring holes into her younger brother. His shoulders sagged as he kept looking at her. Instantly, Simone felt sorry for snapping at him. "Look, after breakfast I promise that I will recover the pictures from the card. Ok?" Jayden smiled and rushed out of the room after giving her a quick hug. Shaking her head, she went to get ready for breakfast.

"So dad, you are not working today?" She asked her father who was on his third cup of coffee as he read the newspaper. Lately, he seemed distressed. She wanted to point it out that it was supposed to be a happy start but he was distressed already. Jayden was having trouble making friends at school and Simone was missing pieces of her memory. She had told her parents about it just this morning and they had shared a look of concern but had said nothing. "Its Sunday. Why would I work on Sunday?" He asked, placing a hand over his heart in mock anguish. "You were working on Saturday." Simone said, snorting. "The position I've been hired for, it had been vacant for three long years. Imagine the work." Her father said, letting out an audible sigh. "That reminds me, when I came over to deliver you the lunch box, I saw a woman. I couldn't see her face but she was dressed in red. Had long sleek hair." Simone asked, twirling her fork in the noodles. "Ah, Madam Mayor. She usually dresses in red or black." Her father said, admiration clear in his voice. "What...what kind of woman is she?" "She is a very good person. Gorgeous and polite. She usually comes in late afternoon with her boyfriend and they work till late at night." Her father said, chugging the remaining coffee in his mug. "Oh. Cool." Simone mumbled as her father ruffled her hair as he left the room.

It took about one hour to recover all the files from the memory card. All the while, Jayden had hovered behind her and thrice she had to tell him to shut up. The camera had not been used since Jayden's trip so when three videos pop up alongside his photos, Simone frowned. They were dated since after they had moved to Elmdale. She couldn't remember recording any. Handing over the files to Jayden, Simone clicked open the first video. Her jaw dropped for what she saw. Shadows in her room accompanied by a woman while she slept. The woman was dressed in red. Even though she had her back towards the camera, Simone could tell that it was the mayor. She saw, horrified, as the woman bent over her and then headed for the camera. She had no idea what she had done to her. When she lifted the camera to do something with it, probably delete the video, Simone gasped and stood up so fast that her chair fell to the floor. Her blood had gone ice cold and her legs were shaking. The woman in the video was someone she knew. It was Brianna Hoskin.

Chapter 7

#7 - Past Incidents

Simone avoided everyone at the school the next day. Trust no one. No one. Just before bed last night, she had stumbled upon her own recording in her phone. She had recorded about her meeting with a guy named Matthew Brown. The guy from the woods. He had told her to be beware. Her missing memories, shadows and her meeting with Matthew made sense but her mind refused to believe any of it.

At school, Simone noticed that Brianna was absent and so were her friends. Where could they be? She wondered as she went from one class to another for the lectures. Nathan had tried to talk to her a couple of times but she had avoided him. She felt bad for treating her only friend that way but the warning made it harder for her to trust him.

When it was off time, she headed straight for the town's library. The building was huge and old. Taking a deep breath, she threw open the door and went inside. There was no one there. Just a couple on the second floor on the table just by the railing. They were laughing over something they were reading from a book. The ground floor, it was quiet. Librarian was busy reading some kind of a magazine.

"Hey..." Simone cleared her throat. Librarian was a middle aged woman with half moon spectacles on her thin nose. She twisted her thin lips, painted red, at Simone as if she was annoyed her presence there. Her bright blue eyes narrowed as she studied Simone. "Oh, you are the new girl." The woman set the magazine aside and clapped excitedly. Simone raised her eyebrow at her dubiously. "Ah..yes. I am.""How can I help you darling?" The librarian chirped. Simone looked at the tag pinned on the woman's breast pocket. Samantha Markson. "Umm I was wondering if there'd be anything about Elmdale in the library." "Oh sweetheart, there isn't much." She said with a wink as she start pressing keys of the computer keyboard. "Why? Isn't this town old?" "It is but not many people stay here. The oldest in Elmdale is a woman aged fifty four atm. Rest just leave. Without a word. I think its the custom here or something." She said with a laugh. "What....?" Simone whispered. What did she mean by people just leaving? "Surprising, I know. I don't know who started the trend but almost everyone leaves a written letter behind for their loved ones before moving out suddenly." Ms. Markson went on, not looking at the Simone's pale face. Did she even realize what she was saying? Why would 'everyone' leave the town like that?

"Ah, found it. Just a few newspaper clippings from the previous few years, nothing new. You might find something interesting since I haven't checked that folder since forever. Elmdale is a small town and hardly anyone knows about it. Except for the people who really know how to look." Ms. Markson laughed, making a face at no one in particular. Simone barely listened to her for her mind was still thinking about the new piece of information she had now. "Here." Ms. Markson scribbled something on a post it note and handed it over to Simone. "To be honest, I'm surprised that you want to know about this town. No one, in my career of eight years here, has asked for the stuff on Elmdale." "Guess there is always a first time for everything." Simone said, looking at the note. Ms. Markson had mentioned the floor, rack and row of the place holding the old newspapers. Mumbling a thanks, she headed upstairs. Sunlight streamed through the old windows of the buildings and illuminated the top floor. Hesitating, Simone looked around for the shadows. She had yet to see them during the day but with the recent turn of events, she had to keep an eye out. She headed for the further corner, away from the couple on the floor. As she went, she kept looking at the shelves and the rare collection of thousands of books. For a small town, Elmdale surely had its collection of books.

At the furthest corner, where the sunlight shone brightest, was a stand with a huge folder on top of it. It was coated with dust. Quietly and smoothly, Simone dusted it off and opened it. She exhaled a bit louder than necessary and tried to calm herself. Her heart was beating furiously in anticipation and fear. The first newspaper clipping was dated back a century. When the town came into be. 1908! It showed a couple of pictures faded with time with description of the town. It was small one. The next few clippings told her about the events, celebrations and few people making it big from Elmdale in politics and sports. Nothing worth important here, Simone thought as she skimmed through the pages. At almost the end she came across a piece of information that caught her eye.A couple mysteriously disappeared from Elmdale. A small town north of Newland. Below the heading, the reporter had mentioned other people that had been missing since the town came into in 1908. There were total of eighteen people missing by the end of 1936.'The disappearance of the inhabitants of Elmdale's continues even after decades. They disappear without a trace. The police and the mayor, Mr. Jason Breckon are concerned regarding this sensitive matter.'

There was nothing after that. Confused, Simone went through all the pages again but there was nothing. At the very end, a newspaper from a decade ago stated that almost sixty people had gone missing in Elmdale but the administration was awfully quiet about it.'I'd like to believe that the people just leave. Move away from the town, leaving their loved ones behind.' The mayor had said in an interview. 'The police and the administration has been working on the cases of missing people for a century but have found no trace. The only explanation that makes sense and we have decided on before closing the case is, people move on. Elmdale is not a big town like all those towns and cities out there in the world so I don't think many people mind leaving.' He had refused to acknowledge the further arguments raised by the people in the years that followed. There was nothing after that. Nothing at all. But the people were still going missing.

Simone was so engrossed at the new information that she entirely missed the darkness spreading through the library. When she felt cold, she jerked up her head to look around her. Shadows. The were crawling through the books and on the walls. She gasped when she felt something cold and slithery on her hand. Shadows were crawling out of the folder she had been reading. What the hell was this? It was her first time seeing them during the day. She took staggering steps back, her scream stuck into her throat. A whimper escaped her lips when she collided with a book rack, sending a couple of books toppling down from the top shelf. The sound of the books landing on the cold hard floor of the library made the shadows stop for a moment. They looked solid. Now that Simone could see them more clearly, she realized that they appeared to be in different shades of black. Some were huge and some were small. Some were disfigured and some looked perfect. They seemed real. They seemed to be breathing. In a way. They oozed eeriness, something that made Simone's heart make desperate spasms. She closed her eyes when they all drew near. Blocking the view behind them to her horror. Solid. Is this the end? She thought as cold crept up her body and she felt the whisper of the shadows' touch.

Chapter 8

#8 - Jenna Collins

"Simone? What are you doing here?" Simone snapped open her eyes at the voice. She looked around her wildly, touched herself to see if she was hurt. No, she was fine and the shadows were gone. As if they hadn't been there. "Hey, you ok?" The voice asked again, concerned this time. Simone looked up to see that it was Nathan. His forehead was creased in worry as he looked at Simone and around her. "What happened?" He asked, edging towards her. "Ahh...." Simone scratched her head, thinking furiously. "I thought I heard a mouse.....I...uh...jumped back and collided into the rack....ummm the books fell and I was scared...that...that...the rack will fall and I'd be trapped underneath it." She finished, nodding and somehow proud of her excuse. Nathan just raised his eyebrows at her.

"What...what are you doing here?" She asked him who was now picking up the books that had fell down on the floor. "I come here a lot. Its the only place that I love to be in." He said, winking at her. After he was done arranging the books, he raked his hand through his hair nervously. "So, anything I can help you with around here?""No

...no. Thank you. I was just...just heading home now." Simone said, making her way towards the stairs. Her legs felt weak and she forced herself to appear composed. Nathan followed her without a word. Downstairs, someone was busy talking with the librarian. Simone could hear her chuckle softly all over to the stairs at the further left of the floor.

"Kyle!! Need to stay?" Nathan called out to the guy from behind Simone, brushing past her towards the main desk."Nah, man. I just followed you here." His friend said, his voice thick as he winked at the librarian. "You're heading home?" Nathan turned to ask Simone. She opened her mouth to say yes but then decided against it."Why?""If you have time, we can go somewhere fun?" He offered, a dimpled smile on his face. Trust no one. No one. Matthew's warning words rang in her head as she looked at the two boys waiting anxiously for her answer."Yeah, I have a little time to wander around. Where do you have in mind?" She asked and cringed a little when Kyle slapped Nathan on the back, sending the poor boy stumbling a couple of steps forward. "Just around the corner. The gaming station." Nathan said, smiling from ear to ear. Behind him, Kyle was rolling his eyes but she could see a hint of smile on his face too. Simone noticed that he was one of the guys who Nathan hung around with most often at school. He had shoulder length brown hair and he was taller than Nathan. Some three to five inches. He even appeared to be older than them. "Isn't that the guys' thing?" Simone said, shaking her head at the idea of boys playing the weird fighting games."Not really. Its the only place around here where the kids hang out often. You'd be surprised to see more girls than guys." Nathan said as they started moving towards the library doors. Trust no one. No one. Simone recalled the warning once more.

"Uh...Do you mind if I drop by my house and change my clothes?" She asked the boys. They both turned around to look at her, then at each other before Nathan nodded. "Thanks. I'll see you here in a few." Simone waved at them awkwardly and rushed towards her bike. Under no circumstances she was going to risk losing her memory of what she had read and saw. Like Matthew had said, she could trust no one. Not even Nathan who had been her only good friend for a month she had been here.

Just outside her house, once again she found Jenna waiting for her. Sighing, Simone walked up to her. "Now, what are you doing here?" She growled out. Jenna just made a face at her before pulling her arm towards the main door. "Whoa wait. What are you doing?" Simone tried to free her hand but failed. "I need to talk to you. Asap!" "We can talk here." "No, we can't. I don't want the shadows to find us." Jenna winked while Simone's eyes widen in surprise. Jenna looked proud of herself. She did not look like she was joking. Simone looked around her, scared that someone might have overheard them but the street was vacant. No one was outside or even in the windows. "I...I don't know what you are talking about." Simone said, her heart beating uncomfortably in her chest. Jenna's lips curved in a taunting smile at her. "Did you really think you are the only who is in search for the answers?" "Look, Jenna, I don't know what you are getting at here."

Simone said, trying to step around Jenna but she stopped her. "I've got to be somewhere."

"I lost my mom a year ago. That is when I realized that there was something wrong with this town. I started noticing things that were off." Jenna said, her voice soft and pain evident from her face. "Please, can we talk inside?" Simone didn't know what to do. Trust no one. No one. The words kept on echoing in her mind. At last, her gave up and beckoned Jenna over. Her father was at work and Jayden was making some kind of project model for his school. Her mother brightened when she saw Jenna with Simone. "Wonderful to see you my dear. What would you like? Ice cream or cold coffee?" "Ice cream maybe?" Jenna grinned, making her mother chuckle.

In her bedroom, Simone kept her distance from her. The videos in her phone which she had recovered from the camera clearly showed that Brianna had needed physical contact with her to wipe her memories away. She was not going to give a chance to Jenna to do the same lest she was lying about everything just to get Simone trust her. They just talked about their classes and classmates while they waited for Simone's mother to bring in the ice cream. "I'm really surprised to see that Nathan spends too much time with you. Mostly he just stays miles away from girls despite them following him around the school." Jenna was saying as she played with her ice cream in the cup. It was gonna melt and ruin her clothes."Look, I don't know what people think but I didn't ask him to follow me around. Heck, I didn't even give him any kind of initiative." "Well, that is the exact thing that attracted him. He is a nice guy, you know. Nicer than tons of people around this town." Jenna slurped on her ice cream, making Simone gape at her. That was one weird way of eating ice cream. When they were done, Jenna folded her black red hair into a bun at the nape of her neck and threw open Simone's closet doors. "Come on. We can't take risks.""Jenna, whatever you've got to say, do it here. I'm NOT going to get into the closet with you." Simone said, folding her arms over her chest defiantly. Sighing, Jenna closed the closet doors and headed to pull the curtains over the windows. She closed the door and every place from where the setting sunlight streamed in through. She turned off the light, creating semi-darkness into the room.

"Like I said, I lost my mother last year. She didn't disappear, she was murdered." She began, sitting down on Simone's bed. Simone took the chair beside the table."I was at home when it happened. I....When I heard my mom scream, I rushed up the stairs. I pounded on her bedroom door which was locked. I had to break it in. That is when I found her body. She was drained of blood. Strange, right?" She asked Simone, hugging a pillow close."Look, if you are going to tell me there are vampires in this down then I'm not going to believe you. I mean, what do you want me to think?" Simone said exasperatedly, throwing up her hands. She should've known that having Jenna over was a bad, bad bad idea."Simone, I know. I know that you've lost your memories and you see them. You see the shadows but you don't re-member seeing them. The demons. They control the shadows. This town, they rule over it." Jenna said, trying to keep her voice upbeat. She was looking unseeingly on the floor. Simone didn't know what to say to her. "Unlike you, I have some sense to keep off their radar.""Or directly under it." Simone muttered. Jenna let out a humorless and self depreciating laugh."You know about Brianna. I'm impressed. It took me months to find the truth about her.""Aren't you scared of her?" Simone asked her. Jenna shook her head and looked at her."No, I'm scared of the mastermind behind her. Demons obey someone. Someone I have yet to find out. Someone who is onto you" She whispered the latter part, her fearful eyes looking at Simone.

So, more character pictures are here. Only Vanessa and Sophie pictures are exactly how I've imagined them. Jenna has more sharp lines and Ian is a little more timid in the story ;)

Chapter 9

#9 - An Unexpected Ally

Simone's jaw dropped. "What are you talking about?" "You know that I'm close to Brianna. I follow her sometimes. Keeping a safe distance between us of course. I saw her....once talking to someone I couldn't see the face of. It was a guy. At the mayor's office. She is scared of him. Kind of. She obeys him." Jenna was saying, her voice barely over a whisper. Simone was confused. "And how is that person after me?" "I heard your name. He said your name. That is all." "It is also possible that Brianna reports everything to him?" Simone suggested and Jenna nodded, sucking on her lower lip. "Simone, when people disappear they dispose of their belongings. Their books, they end up in the library. I went there a number of times but Brianna grew suspicious so I stopped but not before I got my hands on some real stuff." Jenna ended with a wink.

"Real stuff?" Simone asked dryly. "Yeah. Since you went into the library today, I know that you must've read the town's history."

"So, you're spying on me?" Simone said, unable to keep aggression from her voice. "God, can you stop being hostile towards me already?" "Look, under the circumstances I don't trust you." Simone said, raking her hand through her hair. "What if you are one of....of those things out there. How would I know?" "Seriously?" Jenna said, clenching her jaw. "Fine, don't believe but I've got to tell you everything before its too late." "Everything?" "Yeah. As you must've read, all this is going on for about a century. Ever since the town came into. What I found, is that the shadows and demons have been here longer than that." Jenna said, throwing a small worn out diary at Simone at catch. "Wait, what?" "In 1964, there was this guy who got lucky. Like many others over the century, he had noticed that something was off about this place but unlike the others, he actually managed to stay alive for the time being." Simone sucked at her lower lip as she opened the diary. She could see messy handwriting scrawled on the yellow pages. She was afraid that the paper would tear into pieces just at her touch. "What happened to him?" She whispered, fingering the words. "Which happens to everyone else who tries to get too close to the truth." Jenna replied sadly, looking down at her interlocked fingers. "Oh." "So, this guy stated that the presence of these creatures he called demons goes back to before the town came into. They are the result of a curse." Jenna said. "Oh great, a curse now. What's next? Aladdin's magic lamp?" Simone blurted out, immediately regretting the words that had left her mouth. Jenna looked hurt. "Simone, I'm trying to help." "Fine, go on." "Unfortunately, the guy couldn't find out about the origins of the curse or anything else about it.

Though, he did write in his journal that these creatures are bound to something. Means, something is keeping them in here. In this town. I also wondered why they aren't seen outside the town, why in Elmdale so when I found the journal, this explanation made sense." Jenna kept going as Simone was leafing through the pages carefully. She skimmed over the entries and she could tell that the guy had seen worst. She wondered how he had managed to not go crazy? "Does this information also tells about what to do to get rid of them?" She asked, fully aware of her running out of time. Nathan and Kyle must be waiting for her. "Be patient, I'm getting there." "Be quick because Nathan and Kyle would be here any minute now. I bought a few minutes to change my clothes before hanging out for a while." "Wow." Jenna said, blinking at her. Simone didn't know what to take of her reaction. "Anyway, if this guy is right about his claims then it means if we find that particular thing that binds these creatures to the town, by destroying it we can get rid of them. Question is, where are we going to find it and how?" "That's all?" "Getting this much was risky enough Simone. Learn to appreciate a little." "Fine, good job. What else do you want me to do?" She asked, hastily growing through her clothes in the closet. She could not decide. "Help me. Help me set things right or this will keep on happening forever." Jenna pleaded behind her. "Did you also know that you can't leave the town now? Like ever?" She said sadly. Simone stilled. Recalling the warning from the old man the day they had moved into Elmdale. "What?" She croaked out the word. "What did you say?" "Whoever tries to leave Elmdale after living here vanishes." Jenna sounded glum now. "There is no way back so there's got to be someone to take the initiative and destroy these beings."

"You're....you're right." Simone nodded, slumping down on her bed. "And two people are much better than one. Together, we can find out more." Jenna was saying. She reached out to hold Simone's hand. "Ah yes. Ok." "So, are you going to share what you know?" Jenna asked politely, squeezing Simone's hand before letting go. Simone's mind was whirling, piecing together everything she knew. Or she thought she knew. "I don't know much." She mumbled. Compared to Jenna, she really had nothing on her. "I just found out about Brianna and....wait. Do you know the Browns? The people who lived in this house?" She asked, turning to face Jenna fully. "Of course, I do. They vanished. But I know that they were murdered. Why?" Jenna was confused. "Their son, Matthew Brown. Did he die too?" "I don't know, Simone. I really don't." Jenna replied apologetically as she stared at Simone. "I met him." Simone said listlessly. "You....you what?" Jenna stood up, her eyes wide and mouth open. "How is that possible? Browns were murdered three years ago." "Believe me when I say that he is alive. He's been living in the woods." Hoping that she could remember her meeting with Matthew. All she knew was through the recording. "Oh my God. Tell me everything." And so Simone did. Somehow she knew that Jenna was right. She could not deal with this all alone. She needed someone to rely on. After she was done, Jenna held her head in her hands. Before she could say a word, the house bell rang. It was Nathan.

"Look, I gotta go. We'll talk more." Simone said and she hastily changed her shirt into whatever her hands grabbed from the closet. Jenna was still shaking her head. "We'll have to meet up again. So many times I wish that we had phone service in this town." She mumbled as she watched Simone pull her long hair in a ponytail. She did not want her mother to go and answer the door for she did not want Nathan or Kyle to know that Jenna had been at her house. "We will." She promised Jenna and rushed for the main door. Thankfully, her mother was in the kitchen with headphones on while Jayden was nowhere to be seen.

When she stepped out, Nathan and Kyle were there. Both were on their bikes. "Took you long enough." Kyle remarked. "Its ok. No rush." Nathan said after throwing a look at Kyle. Without a word, Simone got onto her bike and her eyes landed on the forest in front of them. Further ahead, the forest was still dark under the bright afternoon sun. "You ok?" Nathan called back to her when he realized that she was not moving. "Yeah, I'm....I'm fine." Nathan kept looking at her as she joined them on the road and then he looked back at the forest. Simone knew she'd hate whatever idea he'd come up with the moment he opened his mouth. "You know what, let's go there." He said mischievously, jerking his head back at the forest. "You know we can't, smartie pants." Simone shot back at the same time when Kyle snapped, "No way, man!"

"What? Learn to live a little Kyle. Come on, Simone. Don't tell me that you're scared." He taunted her, making her groan in protest. Deep down she wanted to go but she was scared too. "Nathan..!!" Kyle said warningly but his friend ignored him. Leaving his bicycle just outside the gate of Simone's house, he grinned at the two of them. "Let's have a race. The one to reach....." Even before he could finish, Simone took off. She ignored when Nathan mockingly accused her of cheating and Kyle shouting to tell her to come back. There was no turning back now. She wanted to visit the forest.

Chapter 10

#10 - Mine

Simone ran. Branches snugged at her clothes and the twigs snapped beneath her feet but she did not stop. She could tell that Nathan was close behind her. The trees started to thin out almost immediately. Surprised, Simone halted midway for there was an open space in front of her. Behind her, Nathan also came to a stop. Both of them were breathing heavily. While Simone looked at everything around them, Nathan bent over with his hands on knees as he took deep breaths.

"Ok, you win." He rasped. "Nathan, look." She whispered instead. Just ahead of an open space, there was a rocky hill which rose even higher than the tallest tree in the forest or so Simone thought. " Wow....Truth be told, I've never be this far in the forest before." He said as he took cautious steps towards what appeared to be a cave at the base of the hill. "Nathan, be careful." She called out to him but he waved his hand at her from over his shoulder. Just then, Kyle appeared behind them, looking like an angry bull. His long hair hand twigs and dried leaves. He looked comical enough to send Simon into fits of laughter. "Oh God. I wish I could show you the way you look right now." She said, pointing at his hair. "Wait till you see where you've come, you idiot." He growled out in response. Simone's laughter vanished at his words.

"Kyle, shut up man! Don't be a coward." Nathan called out to them, beckoning Simone to follow him. She hesitated, recalling her last visit to the forest. What was she thinking? What if she made these guys run into Matthew? She had hoped to lose the boys in the forest and then wait for them to return without her but they had followed her. Almost too perfectly. Suddenly, Simone's throat was dry and her heart thudded in her chest. When they were quiet, they could hear the wind moan through the trees. Just as she watched, the shadows of the trees became deeper. Soon enough, she could see them crawling up on the hill where the sunlight was the brightest. They had appeared twice in one day. During the day. What was going on? "Nathan!!!! WE NEED TO LEAVE!!" Kyle shouted at his friend, not looking up at the shadows above them. Could he see them? Simone thought numbly. "A sec..." They heard Nathan say. "NATHAN!!" She screamed his name when the hill above them started to darken with the shadows. Just how many were there? "Oh my God." Beside Simone, Kyle whispered. His eyes were transfixed towards where Nathan had disappeared. Mist or fog. It was one of those things and it was spreading fast. Nathan was nowhere to be seen. "NATHAN!!!" Simone and Kyle screamed together. "RUN!!" They heard Nathan shout before he appeared from the fog. He was limping and his forehead was covered with sweat drops. "RUN AS FAST AS YOU

CAN!" "WHAT THE HELL IS THIS?" Simone shouted back at him all the while resisting Kyle's grip on her arm. "Mist. It'll make you numb." Nathan was saying, his breathing labored as he had trouble walking. Jerking his hand away, Simon ran to help him. Cold. The mist was cold around her ankles just like the shadows were. She shuddered but the need to help Nathan won over whatever she was feeling. "Let's go." She said, taking his arm and draping it over her shoulders. Nathan jerked back from her. When he gripped her shoulders to make her face him, she could see that his face was red with pain. Why couldn't she feel anything? She wondered. "Just. Go." With these words he pushed her away. She watched, horrified as the mist swallowed him whole. She let out a scream as Kyle began dragging her away. A few steps later, they broke into a run. She ran as fast as she could, ignoring the sharp branches hitting her face. She was sure that she had a couple of cuts on her face and her hands were bleeding.

Soon, they were out of the forest. Kyle stopped a couple of steps ahead of her. He, too, was breathing heavily but otherwise appeared to be in lot better condition than Simone was in. Nathan wasn't there. Was......was he.... "He is not coming back, is he?" Kyle asked her in almost a whisper. Simone had a huge lump in her throat and she did not trust herself to speak. "What's going on here?" She turned at Jenna's sharp voice behind her. So she hadn't left when Simone had. "Nathan......Nathan...he...he suggested going..." Simone stopped, not trusting herself to go on. "Stupid jerk!" Kyle mumbled, pressing heels of his hands against his temples. "Simone, what happened?" Jenna asked once again, her inquisitive gaze meeting Simone's. "Nathan....I think he is gone." It was all Simone could say. Jenna gasped as Kyle kicked a stone in frustration. What were they going to do now? Was Nathan really gone? What exactly had happened back there? Too many questions clouded Simone's mind. When Kyle started walking away, his shoulders sagged and head down, Simone lost all the hope she had. "What....should we...are we supposed to tell anyone?" Simone asked Jenna, not realizing that she was gripping at her t-shirt too tightly. Jenna tried to hold her at an arm distance and shook her once to get her all attention. "Were the shadows there?" She asked Simone. Gulping, Simone nodded and told her about the mist. "Then the demons will take care of the matter. Don't worry." Jenna had said. When she had dragged Simone back to her house, the sun had almost set behind them. When Jenna told Simone to get into the bed, she had obliged. She was too tired and had told her mother that she was coming down with a flu or something. She was left alone to rest.

"After what happened today, I'm sure Brianna or someone else will come to wipe away your memories of today." Jenna whispered, bending down to face Simone who was lying straight and staring unseeingly at the roof. "Let them come. I want to forget. It is my fault. It is." Simone sobbed and bit her cheek to keep herself from crying. She could taste blood. "No, it wasn't your fault." Jenna said softly and went to take out Simone's camera. Turning it on, she set it among her clothes in the closet in such a way that it faced the bed. Simone would've appreciated it all any other day but not today. Not at all. Nathan was gone. She was the one for whom he had suggested visiting the forest. It was her fault. Only hers.

Simone opened her eyes to the sounds of birds chirping outside her bedroom window. Surprised, she threw aside the covers and ran to see. Throwing open the window, she gasped at what she saw. Birds. Lots and lots of them flying from over the Elmdale. What was going on? What had made them fly away from the forest? With her eyes wide, she stared at the forest on her left. Suddenly she recalled the events of the day before. Her legs gave out beneath her and she collapsed on the window seat. Nathan was gone. There had been a mist and and....She ran towards the closet, recalling the camera Jenna had left there. The camera was still there, recording just as Jenna had set it up. What had happened? Why hadn't she lost the memories? She stopped the video and then played it.

Brianna had come. Simone could clearly see her in the video, standing near her bed. She was dressed in all black but her face visible. She was wearing bright red lipstick. When she was about to bend over sleeping Simone, she jerked back in surprise. Someone else had entered the room. Simone's throat went dry as she saw Brianna's face. The demon's mouth was hanging open and her eyes were wide. "What are you doing here? Why did you come here?" The camera had recorded her voice clearly. "Leave her alone, Quinlynn." Said a guy's voice. She could not see him. He must've stood by the door. "Why? Why should I leave her be?" Brianna had snapped. "Because she is mine." The deep voice had replied. Simone gasped as the camera dropped from her hands and onto her bed. Demons obey someone. Someone who is onto you.

Chapter 11

#11 – Confrontation

She ran to Jenna's. Her feet barely hitting the road. She had barely heard her mother calling her for breakfast. When she reached her friend's house, she pounded on door. An old guy opened it up when she was between knocking. He clearly looked annoyed."Jenna, she hasn't left for school, has she?" Simone rasped, breathing heavily. Before she could get a reply, Jenna was there. "Simone, you ok? What...what are you doing here so early in the morning and......." She stopped when she saw the camera in Simone's hand. Suddenly she went tense and rigid."Come...come on in. Gramps, I have something really important to discuss about our history project before school, ok?" Jenna told her grandfather and dragged Simone inside the house. She didn't let go of her hand as they went up the stairs and into Jenna's room. Simone didn't even stop and thrusted the camera at Jenna. Without a word, they re-watched the video. Jenna's hands shook at the part where Simone had dropped the camera."Yours?" Brianna had chewed out the words."Leave, Quinlynn." The deep voice had commanded. The video ended with Brianna disappearing into the thin air.

"This...this is....I told you." Jenna said, putting away the camera."W hat..what do we do now? I mean...I...uh...what did I ever do to attract his attention? Whoever it is." Simone said, rubbing her forearms to ward off the chill. "I don't know Simone, I really don't." Jenna whispered back, still holding the camera. Nodding, Simone took back her camera and left for her house to get ready for the day at school.

"Where have you been? Is everything ok?" Her father asked her just outside the main door. Seeing him all ready for office, Simone had an idea. It was time to face whatever demons lurked in the town. She didn't want to wait and be hunted. "Dad, I have an important message for the mayor. Think you can drop it off at her office?" Her father raised his eyebrow at her, his mouth slightly ajar. "I mean, just slip into her office from under the door. You can do that, right?" Simone added hastily."Honey, if there is any issue regarding anything, you can talk to me or your mom." "No, everything is alright. Its just that there is something I want the mayor to know. I don't want others to find out. Yet." She said with a forced smile.

I've found Matthew Brown, son of Tom and Martha Brown. If you want to meet him, come by Dawsons' house. Alone.

Simone didn't feel too confident after handing over the note to her father. A number of times, she wanted to rush to the mayor's office and take the note back from her father. Seeing Brianna act normal at school didn't help either now that she was alone. Nathan was gone. Everyone for except two people acted as if everything was alright in the world. Kyle joked and talked with his friends. If was clear that he had forgotten everything that had happened in the forest yesterday. Everyone acted as if Nathan Woods had never existed.

"This is insane." Jenna had whispered to her in their literature class. Vanessa and Brianna had thrown her a look, clearly confused at the sudden closeness between Simone and Jenna. When Simone opened her mouth to say more at the matter, Jenna elbowed her and then jerked her head subtly towards Brianna sitting just two seats away. Simone wanted to say that there was no light and there were no shadows. How would Brianna know?

When Simone couldn't take anymore, she went to stand by Nathan's locker. It was her first time standing there. Before, it had always been Nathan waiting for her at her locker. It was unlocked. Simone opened it hesitantly, looking over her shoulders to see if anyone was looking at her suspiciously. No one was. She was sure they all had forgotten about Nathan Woods. He had been wiped from their memories. Simone clenched her jaw and looked inside the locker. It was empty. It was as if it had been empty since forever. "I'm sorry, I can't do it." She whispered and ran out. No one stopped her as she cycled back to her house. Her parents were not at home so she let herself in and rushed to her bedroom where she let her tears flow.

Simone waited for someone, anyone to show up by the forest but no one did. Evening rolled in and her family was back. Jayden's project had been a hit and he was practically glowing. Her parents were proud of him and had decided to take them out for dinner. "I don't want to go. I'm tired." She had excused herself."Simone, I found out that you were absent from a couple of your classes today." Her mother had said, throwing a yellow shirt at Jayden to change into."Yeah, I felt sick and didn't have it in me to go to principal's office for the leave." She mumbled. A lie slipping out easily. Her parents seemed to have bought it which was why, an hour later she was alone in the house. She had turned off the lights of the entire house and had seated herself in the window seat of her bedroom. She waited. The ticking of the clock was the only sound she could hear. Distant sounds of laughter and dishes could barely be heard. Her eyes grew heavy as she waited. She was about to doze off when she heard it. Click, clack, click, clack.... The sound of heels. It sounded familiar. Simone didn't move from her spot. She was afraid that she'd cause a sound.

It was a woman. She stopped in front of the forest, her back to Simone's house. Swallowing, Simone ran. Towards the main door, to confront her. To confront Brianna or Quinlynn. Whatever was her name was.

"Brianna!!" Simone called as she stepped out of her house. Slowly, the woman turned around to look at her. Seeing her face to face made Simone's throat go dry. Beside her, the street lamp flickered. Without even turning to look, she knew that shadows were forming around them. "Well, well. Looks like our smart girl has caught me." Brianna said. Her voice was ice cold which sent shivers down Simone's spine. Around them, everything had stilled or how Simone felt it. She couldn't even feel the evening breeze blowing. "What do you....you want?" Despite herself, she stammered. When Brianna laughed, her eyes glowed ember."I want you to stop being so nosy. I've tried to make your life easy here but now you have dug your own grave." Brianna said as she started walking towards Simone. She oozed confidence and shadows seemed to part ways for her. Simone gulped and took a couple of staggering steps back."You've....you've ....been...killing people." Simone managed to say. Brianna chuckled darkly."Killing? Have you seen me kill, sweetheart?" "No but I know. Everyone who disappears – ""Well, your food does disappear when you eat it." Brianna cut in. "And then you throw away or bury the bones." At these words, Simone stopped breathing and her legs gave out beneath her. Air whooshed out of her lungs when her back hit the road. Brianna laughed boisterously. "You really are smart, aren't you?" "What...what are you going to do to me?" Simone whispered, visibly shaking with fear."What do you think? I hate being challenged and you've challenged me." Brianna said menacingly. Simone's heart pounded with helpless, animal fear with every step Brianna took towards her. Simone glanced behind Brianna, at the shadows waiting. Waiting for what? She did not know. She closed her eyes, regretting sending the note. Regretting everything. She stopped moving back on her hands when she had in the center of the shadow casted by her house. Brianna had stopped walking at just the edge of the shadow.

"If you thought that you'd be safe from the shadows in the shadow, then I should give it to you that you do have common sense. Too bad, it got you here.""Go ahead.....kill....kill me." Simon said, looking up at Brianna. "Awww..." Brianna cooed and then Simone felt herself being pulled. Alarmed, she tried to hold onto anything on the road but her fingers caught nothing. Her nails cracked and were bleeding in seconds. She stopped at Brianna's feet. A sick smile was dancing her lips as she saw crimson drops fall on the road from Simone's fingernails. They bloody hurt but Simone didn't want Brianna to know how much she was hurting."Any last words, darling?" Brianna smiled gleefully, her ember eyes glowing even brighter.

"Quinlynn!!!" A booming voice said behind them. Brianna's smile vanished as she took a step back from Simone to look. Behind her, someone was stepping out into the light from the shadow of the house. Someone Simone knew. "No...." She gasped when the light fell on Matthew's unruly curly hair. The way the shadows vanished at his presence and Brianna's shoulders sagged, Simone knew. Matthew had been the one. He had been the leader, the one the shadows and demons obeyed.

Chapter 12

#12 - Trar'en

"Oh, its you. Fancy you showing up here." Brianna tittered, covering her mouth with her pale hand. "You forced my hand. I told you to leave the girl alone yet here you are." "You know that she is a problem, right? Like all the others, we need to eliminate her." She said, pointing in Simone's direction from over her shoulder. Matthew just tilted his head. "I told you that I will handle her." "I've always done your dirty work Trar'gen. Always. Why is it that this time I can't get my hands dirty?" "Because you've been reckless and impatient. You didn't even know about Mathew Brown for three whole years." Matthew said. Simone frowned. What was he saying? "You were there too, that night. You should've known about him if I didn't." Brianna shot back which made Matthew smile. A sinister smile. "I did. I waited for you to realize your mistake but you didn't." Matthew's words were sliding out with a lazy glee. Nothing was making sense to Simone. She wanted to run back to her house, to the safety of her closet but when she tried to take a step back, she jerked in surprise. Looking down, she gasped in horror. Shadows were pooling around her and gripping onto her legs. "And here you are, wearing his face like a trophy after killing him." Brianna laughed mirthlessly which made Simone's skin prickle with fear.

"I had to because you were not capable of recognizing your error from three years ago. I caught him communicating with my friend over there." Now, Matthew looked up at Simone. Even though they were but a few feet apart, Simone could see that his face held no warmth for her. "All the more reason to get rid of this problem, right here and right now." Brianna intoned, patting Matthew's cheeks as if he were a kid. Almost instantly, Simone felt the shadows crawl up her legs. When she opened her mouth to scream, something cold silenced her. "I didn't say that you can do that." Matthew said softly. Brianna stilled and turned to face him. "What did you say?" "She is not yours to kill, Quinlynn. I really appreciate all the hard work you did to subdue her but I'd like you to hand her over to me." Simone let out a muffled scream and shook her vigorously but the shadows were holding onto her tightly. She couldn't feel her hands or legs anymore. "No. Never. I hate it when you keep secrets from me, do things out of ordinary. I know pretty well how it ended the last time." Brianna said, giving him a sweet smile as she walked around him. Matthew just chuckled in response. "You know you can't fight me, Quinlynn. Give up." "Never, sweetheart." Brianna whispered into his ear from over his shoulder before her eyes caught Simone's. Simone couldn't breathe and she closed her eyes. Praying desperately. She felt herself being pulled smoothly.

It all happened like a thunder flashing in the sky. One moment Simone was being choked and frozen to death, the next moment she felt herself thrown back. Horrified, she opened her eyes. Shadows were diving to catch her. Behind them, she could see Quinlynn, her face all contorted in concentration. Simone let out a scream. She was going to hit the road beneath her and die. Just like that. "QUIN-LYNN!!" Somewhere close to her, Matthew roared. His voice total unhuman. Just before Simone could hit the ground, arms reached out to catch her as smoothly as if she had slipped not threw back into the air some good fifty feet. It was Matthew. He had saved her. Before Simone could comprehend what was going around her, shadows closed in. She thrashed in Matthew's arms but he held her close. His grip was ice cold on her warm skin. When the shadows formed a blanket over them, she struggled to breath. Her lungs screamed at the lack of oxygen. She could not breathe. "Ma....ma..." She tried to call Matthew but failed. She gave up fighting then and welcome the darkness that clouded her mind.

Cold. She felt something cold around her ankles and around her wrists. Shadows. She snapped open her eyes only to gasp in alarm. She pulled at her arms and legs but they didn't budge. She was tired down with iron chain. On a chair. Thankfully, her mouth wasn't taped. She screamed. "SOMEONE!!" She called but heard no response. She had no idea how long she cried and screamed before she collapsed back into the chair, tired. Only then she allowed herself to examine the room she was in. It was some kind of basement with a staircase just a foot behind her while a chair and a table adorned corner of the room. In the corner on Simone's right, there was a small bed. So she was locked up. Where? She did not know. With her head heavy and eyelids aching with all the crying and screaming, Simone let herself drift off to sleep.

When Simone came around again, she was lying down on something soft but she still could feel something cold around her one ankle and wrist. She cursed and opened her eyes. "You're alive." She looked up at Matthew's voice. He was leaning against the table with his hands in his pants' pockets. He looked at ease but officious at the same time. At the sound of his deep voice coming from the mouth of the boy she knew, she shuddered. "Where am I?" She managed to ask in a whisper, her eyes trained on the roof or what appeared to be. No, it wasn't the roof but the shadows. Shadows all over her head. "It's the place where we keep the people before killing them off. People who are too troublesome to bet let out in Elmdale." He replied calmly. "What do you plan on doing with me?" "As of now, nothing. What I am and what I want, you will need time to be willing to listen to it all. I believe now is not the time." He said, his voice fading away. "WELL, IT IS TIME YOU MONSTER." Simone shouted, facing the table but he was gone. There was no one. Above her, she shadows moved before going still again.

For the next few days or hours, she could not tell, Simone kept drifting in and out of sleep. Sometimes she saw Matthew but he barely ever said more than a word or two. He had freed her wrist but one of her ankles was still chained to the iron bed. Simone had tried to move it but it didn't even budge. Simone was fed too. She never saw who brought her the meals but she had her ideas. All she saw in the room she was in shadows. Everywhere. They never touched her but seemed to be keeping a watch on her. She had tried talking to them, shouting at them but it barely got a reaction out of them. Then one day, Matthew brought her food tray himself.

"How long are you going to keep me here?" She asked him, eyeing the meat balls and spaghetti on the tray. "Till you are ready to listen to me and believe me." He replied, his cold deep voice making her shudder. He was scary, no matter how harmless he appeared to be. There was this aura around him which made her feel that he wasn't someone she could mess with. "Look, you are keeping me locked up here with creepy shadows all around. If you expect me to believe you and trust you then you are mistaken." She shot back, sending bits of her food from her mouthful. A disgusted looked passed over his face before it became passive once more. "Did you know that we were created with a curse?" Instead of reply, Simone nodded vigorously. "A curse casted for revenge. A curse that doomed the people of Elmdale for eternity." Matthew had started pacing around the table as he talked. "Who...why would someone do that?" She found herself asking. "For revenge. Man goes too far for revenge. He is blinded by it and eventually, it destroys him." Matthew was looking up at the shadows now.

"Shadows, are they also result of the curse?" "No. We are the creatures of darkness, we summoned them to be our eyes and ears." He said, looking down at her from over his shoulder. An amusing smile was playing in his lips but his eyes were calculating, evil. Simone looked away.

"You are not Matthew Brown, are you?" Simone asked, a huge lump forming in her throat once more. "No, I'm not." "Then who are you, really?" She whispered, afraid to know the answer. With the way he smiled, her heart went cold. "Someone you know very well." No, no, it couldn't be. "Show me your real face." She asked him, closing her eyes and praying desperately. When she opened them, she let out a sob. It was Nathan Woods.

Chapter 13

#13 - Purpose

Simone let out a scream. "HOW COULD YOU?" She shouted at him and thrashed against the chain holding her to place. Nathan just tilted his head and regarded her. Gone was the warmth from his face and his usual dimpled smile. How could this monster be her friend for more than a month now? How could he be the one she had trusted and considered a friend? "YOU ARE LYING, YOU PATHETIC MONSTER!!" She screamed once more. The chain refused to free her. It just rattled against the iron bed. "Simone, I care for you. If I hadn't, you wouldn't have been here." Nathan said generously when she quieted down. She was breathing heavily and her arms hurt. She didn't want to see his face. For a moment, she thought she'd be able to remember who Nathan had been instead of the person standing before her. "I will never hurt you, rest assured." "What about the people I love? What about the people of this town?" She snarled, still avoiding to look up at him. She heard him sigh before she felt the mattress compress under his weight beside her. She hid her face behind her loose hair. "We are cursed to feed on the people of this town." He said softly but his voice still sounded unconcerned. With her heart sinking, Simone recalled how it had always been like this but she hadn't noticed. "Without...without harming them, there is no way we would survive." "Then die!!" Simon shot back with her clenched teeth. "That's what I'm planning to do." At Nathan's words, she stilled. What was he talking about? "But I can't just go without taking down Quinlynn and Juniper." He kept going. Now, Simone dared to turn around and look at him. He was looking unseeingly at something on the opposite wall. His hands indifferently caught a ball to and fro.

"How can I trust the words you are saying?" "Whether you like it or not, I'm still the same Nathan you've known for more than a month now." He replied calmly before he stood up to leave. Simone closed her eyes, anger flaring through every inch of her. Above her, she shadows shuddered and went still once more.

Thwack! Someone slapped her cheek, hard. Startled, Simone shrieked as she opened her eyes and saw Quinlynn bent over her. "Oh, there she is." Quinlynn said in a sing song voice. When she stepped back, Simone gasped in shock. Vanessa was standing against the wall by the door. The girl just smiled at her with her pointy teeth. Beside her, two girls stood still. Their eyes were vacant and bodies lifeless. They looked like they were in a daze. "What's....what's going on here?" Simone asked, her eyes wildly traveling from one girl to the other. Her heart was thudding and her veins buzzing. What was Quinlynn up to?

"I'm sure Trar'en fancies you, you know but before you day dream about being safe and all, I wanted to show you something." Quinlynn chuckled, pacing around Simone's bed. "What?" "You see, Trar'en hasn't fed for a long time now. I'm sure he is low on his energy. Above you is the proof enough." Quinlynn winked before looking up. Following her gaze, Simone looked up. The shadows were shuddering. As Simone watched, one by one they fell like rain drops. Startled, Simone recoiled but she didn't feel cold. No shadow touched her. She dared to open her eyes at Quinlynn's gleeful laugh. The shadows were nowhere to be seen.

"He is weak and he dares to save you. From me." Quinlynn said, bending to level her face with Simone's. She was wearing bright red lipstick and heavy make-up. She looked unnervingly beautiful. Simone was afraid of her nonetheless. Very very afraid. "We've followed Trar'en for centuries but now, we believe that he is not capable of leading us. I've stood by him all this time, I stood by him even when he killed two of ours in cold blood." Quinlynn actually sounded a little sad. When her long, red painted nail touched Simone's temple, she shrunk back. With a smile, Quinlynn tucked loose strands of Simone's hair behind her ear. "I'm gonna show you something cool. Watch carefully." Quinlynn whispered. Before Simone could ask her anything, she heard footsteps beyond the door and then door being thrown open. She wasn't surprised to see Nathan there. His eyes were glowing bright ember, the only sign that he was furious at Quinlynn's presence in the room.

"Oh hello darling! We've been waiting for you." Quinlynn cooed as she sashayed towards him. Without even moving a finger, he sent her flying into the wall. Quinlynn managed to catch herself before she hit it. Vanessa faced Nathan, to protect her friend. He made no move against her though. When he shouldered past her, Simone knew why. He had made her immobile. Shadows, darker than the usual ones were holding her in place. Her arms were pinned to her sides. "I didn't know you could become so pathetic!" Quinlynn said, pushing her tight skirt down and flicking her black hair over her shoulder. "I'm afraid I can't say the same about you. You've always been pathetic, reckless and impatient." Nathan said calmly, facing her with his hands in his pants' pockets. Quinlynn let out a mirthless laugh. "But not stupid, sweetheart." She said before she pushed one of the girls into the wall just like Nathan had done with her moments ago. Simone let out a whimper in fear and alarm as she heard a couple of bones crack.

The effect was almost immediate. Simone realized with horror what Quinlynn was aiming at. Nathan groaned as he hunched over, his hands pressed against his temples. He groaned in pain which made Quinlynn clap with triumph. "Come on, go ahead and feed. Show that little girlfriend of yours what you truly are." "Get....Get....lo...lo st Quinlynn!!!" Nathan moaned, collapsing on his knees on the floor. "Oh baby, you can't do anything to make it possible." She just chirped in response. With a flick of her finger, Vanessa was free. "Stop fighting it, Trar'en. You can't deny who you truly are." Vanessa said, lifting the girl who had hit the wall from the back of her shirt. She pushed the girl in front of Nathan who jerked back as if struck by lightning. His face looked horrible. It was pale and he was shaking. "Oh come on! Stop wasting the time fighting what you want most." Vanessa tutted. Quinlynn practically pushed the girl's face towards his. Simone saw fight leave Nathan as he fixed his eyes on the girl. When he placed his hands on the girl's temples, net-black veins appeared on every visible part of his body. Simone choked with terror when she noticed blood being drained from the girl's body. Nathan's eyes were closed but he looked like a monster. What he truly was. Simone welcomed the darkness that seemed to overtake her mind. It was too much. She could not handle it.

She was trapped. No, someone was holding her. And running. She snapped open her eyes only to find herself looking right at Nathan's face. The image of him with black veins on his body was sudden. She shrieked and he let her go in alarm. Simone fell on the ground with a thud, sharp branches and stones pressed against her body, making her scream. "I'm sorry. You startled me." Nathan was saying. When he reached out to lift her up, she batted his hands away. "Get away from me, you monster!!" "Simone, you need me right now." He replied impatiently. Groaning, Simone struggled to stand up straight. Her legs betrayed her though, they gave out under her and she fell on the floor once more. When Nathan made no move to come near her, she let herself study her surroundings. They were in the forest and the sun was setting. With a sinking feeling, she realized that he was taking her to where he had disappeared the last time. When he had been pretending to be hurt and had vanished in the mist. She looked at him with a clenched jaw. How could he toy with her trust? Oh, he was a monster.

"Why did you bring me here? To kill me where no one can know?" She growled. Rolling his eyes, Nathan sat down on a tree log. He narrowed his eyes as he regarded her. "Like I said, I'm not going to hurt you. The only reason I've brought you here is that...help me break this curse on the town." "How is that advantageous for you?" Simone stated bluntly. A look of hurt passed over Nathan's face even before she could register it being there. "It'll set me free." "Set you free as in you'd be free to roam the Earth and drain people of their blood?" A hint of derision coloring Simone's tone. Nathan just gave her a smirk. "No, free as in to kill us for once and for all." Simone's eyes widen. He was planning to kill himself and the other two. She opened her mouth to say that she did not believe him and that he was only toying with her but got distracted.

Behind him, she saw shadows rise. They were darker and bigger than Simone had seen up till now. Wind moaned through the trees. Following her gaze, Nathan looked back and jumped up. He ran towards her and shook her shoulders to get her attention. "Simone! Listen to me carefully." He said. "You are the only one that can make it happen. Destroy the dagger in the cave I took you near once before. Destroy it and set us free." "Why?" Simone whispered, her body visibly shaking from fear of oncoming shadows. "Because I'm the creature of darkness which dreams of the light. And because I've began to care."

Chapter 14

#14 - The Curse of Elmdale

He had spent years studying this particular craft. He wanted to avenge the wrong that had been done to him. "You have outlived your usefulness, my dear. It is time that you leave and go to where you truly belong." She had whispered in his ear. "I belong with you in the palace, your highness." He had said from where he was kneeling on the floor. "No, you do not. My father brought you from the slumps and there you shall return to." "Please, I beg thee. My lady, if I have committed a crime, punish this servant of yours however you deem fit but do not send me back." He had pleaded to her but she had just laughed at him. What had he not given her? Everything just to make sure that she sit on the throne which had been her rightful place since forever. He was a faithful soldier and had stood by the princess all along. Was this how he was going to be repaid? Now that she had her lands back because of all the hard work he had put into every plan, she was discarding him.

The day had finally come. He drew a pentagram on the ground, humming a beautiful melody he had come up with himself. He sprinkled red stone dust on the boundary followed by spider's eyes in each triangle of the star and finally, in the center he placed her dagger. Her beloved dagger which her soldiers were searching around in the lands. After he was done, he waited. When the moon was high above in the sky and the wind moaned through the trees around him, he started chanting. Soon, creatures emerged at each point of the star. Five creatures wearing the skin of human beings. He cackled at the sight of them. "Now, you shall feed on the people of this land forever." He had clapped in excitement as the creatures had stared at him. They were hauntingly beautiful. "Till when, sire?" One of them intoned. "Till this dagger is destroyed but rest assured, you cannot destroy it but only a human can. The one who will care for you despite knowing who you truly are. Someone who descends from the very line of Margret Aurora Throckmorton, the woman who stole it all away from me. It shall never happen. You all will see to that."

Nathan was pulling at her hand and she was trying not to trip over the fallen branches. The shadows were closing in behind them. She swore that she could hear Quinlynn's laughter carried over by the wind. When they reached the spot till where she had come the last time she had been in the forest, Nathan stopped. She was breathing heavily but Nathan was perfect. As if he hadn't ran through the uneven forest ground. Just as Simone had expected, the mist started to form beneath the bushes as they watched. "From here on, you have to go alone. That mist.....it burns us." Nathan said, letting go of her hand. Her heart was stammering in her chest and she bit inside of her cheek really hard. She wanted it to be a dream and wanted to wake up all perfect and normal. But it wasn't a dream for she tasted blood. "Simone, you need to hurry. I'll try my best to hold back the shadows but I can't promise you that I'd be able to do it for long." Nathan said urgently. Taking a deep breath, she started for the cave entrance just beyond the shrubs. The mist did not hurt her. It was just cold. She hesitated. When she turned to look over at Nathan from over her shoulder, she saw that he was already fighting off the shadows with his own but his were weak and no match for Quinlynn's and Vanessa's combined.

"How can I trust you?" She shouted, voicing her concern. "Fine. Don't trust me but trust the Nathan you knew a month ago." He shouted back without even looking at her. Clenching her hands into fists, she started for the cave entrance now barely visible because of all the mist. Her walk to the entrance wasn't easily. Due to mist, she could not see properly where she was going. Twice she slipped but by sheer luck managed to not get hurt. Soon she was stepping into the cave. It was quiet. So quiet that she could hear her own uneven breath. It was dark too and she cursed herself and Nathan for not thinking everything through. The narrow passage started to widen as she kept walking. Somewhere, she could hear water trickling. Soon she could see orange glow up ahead. She rushed towards it. The passage way opened up to a wide space. Rough rocks jagged out from the walls and floor of the cave alike. There was a fountain. A small one in the dead center. On that fountain was a dagger. Its hilt was bright red with blue jewels. The orange glow emanated from the water of the fountain. She could not see the source of it. As she slowly stepped towards the fountain, her heart started beating faster. Her hands were slick and she could feel her shirt stick to her back.

"So, he's really busy." Simone jumped back in shock at Quinlynn's voice. She was standing in the shadows, wearing black and her arms folded over her chest. She had a cruel smile on her face and her eyes were glowing ember. "Cat got your tongue?" She snarled. "What ...how?" Simone staggered back a step. Nathan had told her that it wasn't possible for him to cross the mist. That it burns him but how did Quinlynn managed to pass it? Unscathed at that. "He must've told you that the mist burns him." Quinlynn said, gracefully stepping down to the floor. "He is weak. Can't blame him." "What...do you want?" "You think I don't know what Trar'en is trying to do?" Quinlynn said loftily. "And he dares to think that he can succeed." Simone's heart twisted painfully in her chest. She was going to die, she knew it. Quinlynn stopped right in front of her, her head tilted as she regarded Simone. "Who is going to save you now, sweetheart?" Quinlynn raised her hands as Simone tried to step away but her limbs betrayed her. She could not move. A whimper stuck in her throat as her eyes fell on Quinlynn's hands. Holes. There was gaping holes in the palm of her hands and from those holes, she could see needle like......teeth? Quinlynn smiled mockingly. Simone closed her eyes.

Suddenly, Quinlynn shrieked. Simone opened her eyes to find her flying away into the far wall of the cave. Surprised, she turned to find Nathan just at the mouth of the passage way. His skin, it was red and she could see a number of scars on his face. They were healing slowly. "I'm going to save her, Quinlynn. Don't you get ahead of yourself?" "Where....is Juniper?" Quinlynn growled as she stood up on her feet. Simone could see blood trickling down from the left temple. "Oh, Juniper?" Nathan mocked. Behind him, shadows formed. They were lighter than before. Nathan was running out of his strength. "Here she comes." He raised his hand behind him and folded his fingers into a fist. Around him, the shadows moved. Within a blink of an eye, there was something at his feet. No, it was someone. Vanessa. Burned black.

"NOOOOOO!!!!" Quinlynn wailed. "HOW COULD YOU?" "We've lived long and fed on enough people. Its time that we stop." Nathan said, stepping from over what remained of Vanessa's body. Shaking, Simone retched. "WHY DO YOU CARE? YOU TRAI-TOR!!" With these words, Quinlynn flew towards Nathan and pushed him back with enough force that he flew and hit the wall behind. Simone tried to hide herself behind one of the rocks. Her attempt made a sound which attracted Quinlynn. In a second, she was holding Simone up with the collar of her shirt. Simone struggled to breathe. "Its all because of you, you stupid girl." Quinlynn said through clenched teeth. Her eyes were burning. "Let her go, Quinlynn. This is between you and me." "Is it?" She asked, knocking Simone against the rock she was trying to hide behind. On the contact, Simone's breath whooshed out of her lungs and she collapsed. It hurt. She felt as if her back bone had been shattered into pieces.

"SIMONE!! GET UP!!" Somewhere, Nathan was shouting at her. "GET UP!!" But Simone could not.

Chapter 15

#15 - Free At Last

"Simone, Simone wake up!!" Someone was patting her cheek. She groaned before forcing her eyes to open. She was still in the cave, lying down on the uneven cave floor with her head in Jenna's lap. Jenna? What was she doing here? Simone sat bolt upright. "Jenna." She rasped. Her throat was dry. "Hurry, do something." Her friend pleaded with her and then looked at something behind them. Simone followed her gaze. Nathan. He was badly wounded and he could barely stand up. Quinlynn was unharmed. As the girls watched, she span on her heel and gave Nathan a kick which sent him knocking into the wall. Then, he did not get up.

"You've taken everything away from me. Juniper, Jordan and Sebastian. You killed them." She was saying as she lifted Nathan up from the ground by collar of his shirt. He tried to pry her hand off himself but he was too weak. With Jenna's help, Simone stood up and looked around to find anything, something to help Nathan. The dagger. It still laid in the center of the fountain. She had to destroy that. She jerked her head towards it, silently telling Jenna where to go.

"I don't know what you see in these pathetic human beings or why do you even care." Quinlynn was snarling at Nathan who had his eyes closed. He was in a lot of pain and somehow Simone felt sorry for him. With Jenna's help, she rushed to towards the dagger. Their movement caused Quinlynn to send Nathan flying on the other wall while within a blink of an eye she was right in front of Jenna. "And what do you think you are doing?" "Stop it, Brianna." Jenna said, caustiously stepping back from her. "Stop what? Did you really think I would never find out about you?" "Well, you didn't. Not really which is why I'm here with most of my memories intact. At least the ones that matter." With these words, Jenna pushed Quinlynn and ran towards Simone. Bracing herself, Simone stepped into the water of the fountain. It was cold but not cold enough to numb her body. Still, she felt pin pricks on her skin which was in the water. She gasped due to pain.

Behind her, she heard Jenna scream. "NO!!!" Simone shouted when she turned her head to see her friend. Quinlynn had Jenna up in the air from her hair. Jenna was crying as Quinlynn laughed cruelly. "You're as pathetic as rest of your kind. Think you are the best?" "Quinlynn!!! LET HER GO!!!" Simone shouted, clenching her fists. It made Quinlynn laugh even harder but she does let Jenna go. Simone's friend landed with a thud on the floor and screamed due the pain caused by rocks pressing against her body.

"You think you can win? Do you even know how to destroy the dagger?" Quinlynn intoned as she walked around the fountain. She could not step into it, Simone realized. "Nathan did give me overview of the curse. Only someone who cares about you can destroy it." "And you think you are the one? Who cares about us?" Quinlynn asked, bending down to pick up a pointed rock. She could not step into the fountain but she could throw something. With exact preciosn, she could even kill Simone without touching her. Without giving her any reply, Simone dived for the dagger just when Quinlynn aimed the stone where she had been standing. Her feet were numb. They could not move fast enough. No, it wasn't just her feet. The numbness was travelling up her legs. Simone gave it all she had as she stretched her hand to pick up the dagger. Just when Quinlynn was about to target her again, Nathan threw himself at her. Quinlynn let out a inhumane howl.

"SIMONE HURRY!!" Nathan shouted. As soon as she touched the dagger, everything stilled around her. It was as if the time had stopped itself. Quinlynn was about to strike Nathan but she looked nothing more than a shadow. Nathan was about to throw his arms over his face and Jenna was struggling to sit up.

As Simone watched, shadows rose from the floor of the cave. One of them was larger and more menacing than the rest. Its eyes, they glowed red. Terror stabbed in Simone's heart like a hot poker. "Is it you who seek to destroy an ancient curse on this land?" She shadow boomed. Simone swallowed painfully, unable to look away from its eyes. Around her, everything was just dark. She could not see Jenna or the other two. "Yes." She croaked out the word. "Why?" The shadow asked. Why? Simone pondered over the question. Wasn't it because Nathan had pretty much ordered her to do it? No, it wasn't only that. She wanted to protect the people of Elmdale from the monsters who had been feeding on them for centuries. But it wasn't the entirely reason. She realized that she cared for Nathan. She did want to help him. Simone looked up at the shadow, directly matching his gaze. "Because I care." She whispered. "Dip the dagger into the water of this fountain and recite these words. Chanomai daimonas, adetos tous. " "Greek." Simone whispered. "Who are you?"

"We are the shadows bounded to this dagger. For centuries we've seen the demons raise our kin for their selfish purposes right from this fountain." The shadow replied. His loss was evident from his tone. "How?" Simone was confused. "By throwing in the people they fed on as sacrifices."

With these words, the shadows were gone. Dagger was warm in her hands and everything started moving again.

When Simone turned to look what was happening behind her, she gasped. Nathan was cowering on the floor, shadows streaming out from around him. Simone noticed mist too. It must be burning him, she realized. After ensuring that Nathan was as good as dying, Quinlynn headed towards Jenna. She had not seen what Simone was up to yet. Her back was towards Simone.

Simone looked at Nathan once more. His eyes were pleading with her to hurry. Mouthing 'goodbye', Simone plunged the dagger into the water. She heard a hissing sound as if it had been burning hot. Then she recited the words. The effect was immediate. Quinlynn screamed and rushed towards the fountain but she collapsed midway. She was withering in pain and clawing at her face. Around them, the shadows were screaming. Only then Simone dared to step out from the fountain. Jenna was looking around wildly, her face pale and eyes wide. Simone rushed to her friend and helped her up. Slowly, Quinlynn's body began to disintegrate. Jenna pulled at Simone's sleeve. "What?" "Look." She pointed towards the fountain. The shadows were disappearing into it. A few feet away from the fountain, Nathan was awfully still. Simone ran to him. He was barely breathing and his burned skin wasn't healing. Gingerly, Simone lifted his head into her lap. "You've suffered enough." She whispered to him. Strangely, a huge lump formed in her throat. Beside her, Jenna was awfully quiet. Slowly, all the orange glow was disappearing from the cave. The water was drying. Nathan's body started to disintegrate as well. "Oh God." Simone cried softly. "Thank....you." Nathan said, his voice barely over a whisper. He could barely open his eyes. In them, Simone saw his gratitude towards her. Slowly and painfully, he raised his hand to touch her cheek. "Live....Happily." Trying not to cry, Simone nodded. "You are free." She whispered as Nathan's hand dropped and his eyes closed. Within seconds, his body turned into ashes in her hands and was blown away towards the fountain. Her hands were empty.

Simone woke up to the sounds of birds chirping and her brother banging on her bedroom door. Throwing it open, she scowled. "Are you insane?" "You won't believe it." Jayden said, his eyes wide. "Believe what?" "This town is in uproar. About all the people who left mysteriously, everyone suddenly recalled that they were murdered. By whom, they don't know."

Simone swallowed and shoved Jayden out of the room. "This town is weird." She said before slamming the door close at his face. She rushed to the window and threw it open. There were birds chirping in the trees and squirrels climbed up into them. People were bustling about, looking confused or hysterical. With her heart heavy, Simone closed the window. Her eyes landed on the camera that was resting on her table. She hadn't left it there.

"Hey." It was Nathan in the video. Simone sagged down on her bed as she saw what he had left. "When you'll be watching this, hopefully I'd be long gone. I sincerely want to thank you for helping me out and helping everyone out in Elmdale. I've lived for centuries and I've done every bad thing you can think of. But all is done and I can't change it. Go to Quinlynn's house. You'll find a trapdoor in her living. It leads to a secret floor in the basement. I hope that you'd find some of the missing people alive. I really hope so. One more thing, thirty years ago there was this family Quinlynn murdered. Only six year old girl was spared. Her name was Sophie Throckmorton. I had given her to the old man you saw outside the town. I'm sure you must've seen him. Anyway, connect the dots and live well. Thank you, my friend." Nathan ended with a wink. The video went blank and Simone realized that her cheeks were wet because of the tears.

Outside, the clouds thundered in the sky. She jumped up in surprise when her phone rang from her closet. It was her best friend Nina from her old school. It was working. There were telephone signals all over the town. Smiling, she got dressed. It was time to visit Jenna and go on a rescue mission.

CPSIA information can be obtained
at www.ICGtesting.com
Printed in the USA
BVHW030842091122
651450BV00013B/694

9 781804 779378